This novel is dedicated to those who are willing to see through the deception and question it.

We are the ones who will never fly

Who live beneath the camera eye

And throw ourselves into the race

An invisible army with no face

Prologue

October. 2029.

It felt like he'd been running for hours. His middle-aged body, overweight and enfeebled from years of good living, had tired quickly. A decade of indulgences and rewards offered only to men in his position now weighed heavily on prematurely wasted muscle and bone, each breath that rasped from his depleted lungs a painful testament to a lifetime's addiction to high tar cigarettes. The first stabs of a stitch had developed early, gnawing deeply at his side, their reach deep and unforgiving.

The forest surrounding him was darker than he remembered it being in his childhood, the pathway trodden so many times as a boy now overgrown and undefined. Glancing back over his shoulder, he spat the bitter metallic taste from his mouth, the action causing him to stumble, the loss of momentum bringing him to his knees. As blind panic descended upon him, he felt the telltale constriction of his airways, and for a moment feared he was on the point of blacking out. He waited, hunched over like a wounded animal, his forehead pressed against the cool earth as he willed the worst to pass.

Was it too late to turn back? Was there even the remotest possibility that his disappearance could have gone undetected? He immediately dismissed the thought. He'd been gone for hours; returning was no longer an option. The absence of certain papers and downloaded files concealed in the rucksack upon his back would, by now, also have been discovered. Within hours, he would officially be declared a fugitive—a threat to national security, and branded a danger to the public.

It was a situation no longer in his control. The decision he'd made was an irreversible one, and as such, he would have to see it through to its conclusion. Having witnessed first-hand the levels to which his administration would stoop in their endeavours to destroy someone both financially and socially, he was well aware of the consequences. Truth be known, he had—on more than one occasion—been implicit in the character assassination of a fellow human being. Not that his motives were ever personal ones, but rather carried out in an official capacity.

There was little doubt that any available resources at their disposal would be used to publicly denounce him—his disloyalty to his government embellished and twisted into 'crimes against the people'. He would be paraded in the media, with the sole intention of transforming him from a respectable businessman into a figure of derision and hate. What sort of man was he anyway, to abandon a wife and teenage child to fend for themselves, forcing them to contend with the backlash his transgression would surely bring?

The reality was that a world he'd played a small yet significant role in shaping, was also one which very rapidly began to feel like a noose around his neck. Surely it wasn't possible to have done the things he had, and to escape retribution? Was there really no way to reverse the misery his greed and vanity had brought to others? At nights he would turn fitfully in his bed, his dreams rampant with dark and guilt-ridden thoughts, leaving him exhausted and depressed the following day. At other times he would find himself just standing in his garden, gazing upwards to the skies, unsure of why he was looking there. In his tormented imagination he could feel a kind of malevolent entity wrapping itself around him, while above, an ungodly bird of prey circled, watching him, judging him . . . waiting.

He'd not meant for the project to take the direction it had, and in fairness, his diminishing control of the situation was not entirely his doing. He'd always considered himself an honourable man; anyone who knew him would surely testify to that? Whatever the outcome, his intentions had—at least for the most part—been ethical.

It had all seemed so promising in the beginning, like the dawning of a new age. And yes, he would admit to his becoming swept up in it all, there was no disputing that. But then again, who wouldn't? Only those who have ever experienced power could truly appreciate just how intoxicating it could be, and he'd embraced it with a passion.

Slowly he got back to his feet, allowing his body a few seconds to steady itself before setting off again, his pace less frantic than before, his step a little more cautious. And then, for the first time ever, he heard it—a humming which seemed to rise and fall as it weaved its way towards him through the trees. He was heading in the right direction. All would be okay—yes, he could do this. There was always a solution to any situation, however desperate. A final grab for self-preservation. Spurred on by this thought, he pushed himself onward with grim determination, eager to reach the source of the sound before darkness fell.

With every step he took, the noise was increasing in volume, gradually becoming more aggressive until it had mutated into another; one which was carried on a frequency so low and intrusive that to shut it out was impossible. Lifting his hands to his ears made little difference apart from slowing his progress, and consequently would only increase the chances of him falling again. No—he couldn't afford to take the risk, having come this far. Reluctantly he lowered them to his side once more, concentrating on the path ahead.

At last the forest started to thin, permitting the remnants of daylight to push their way through. By now, the shadows were becoming long and the air a little cooler; beneath his feet, the soil was noticeably firmer. Stumbling out of the undergrowth and into the open fields, he again attempted to block out the noise, but to no avail. Without the trees to filter them, the shockwaves were brutal—angrily pounding away at him, their impact sending tremors down through his bones and into the ground below. He shook his head as though to clear his mind of the chaos within. And then, as his eyes regained their focus, he could only stare, open-mouthed in awe . . .

Barely a quarter of a mile away from where he now stood, it reached out across the landscape for as far as the eye could see. At least two hundred feet high, there was an unearthly, almost spectral quality to it which was both mesmerising and terrifying. Only the orange arcings of escaping electricity contributed any colour to the otherwise washed-out monochrome, spreading outwards from their source like the branches of a tree, before dying away again as quickly as they had materialised. Even from this distance he could smell the high-voltage current which crackled within it, before being spat out as electrostatic discharge, to float across the field around him like some acrid fog.

Like everyone else, he'd seen the Containment Walls from a distance, but had never ventured this close before—until today there was never a reason to. Now, standing overwhelmed before it, he had the feeling of being in the presence of some supreme being; a force he could not begin to understand, let alone control.

Bile began to rise in his throat, hot and acidic. He fought for breath, each gasp feeling as though it would tear the lungs from his chest. *Is this my death?* The thought screamed at him from inside his head, and strangely he was okay with it. Kneeling down on the damp grass, his body finally surrendered itself to the inevitable. Closing his eyes, he rolled onto his side, curled himself into a ball, and waited for whatever form his demise would take. As he lay there, he asked himself how he would be remembered. What words would they engrave into his tombstone?

HERE LIES A NEGLECTFUL HUSBAND

Even he would have to admit to the first two—they couldn't very well be denied. Others in his wake would very likely testify to the third.

And then the worst passed. The pain began to recede; once again he was able to stand. From somewhere deep within, he found an inner strength and resolve, unaware his bladder had let him down, oblivious to the spreading dampness. Now walking forward, he was suddenly conscious of how naked and vulnerable he felt out in the open. For certain, the shelter previously provided to him by the trees was the one reason he'd been able to successfully avoid detection from the satellites. However, by now his location would have been picked up and bounced back to the appropriate authorities. How long before their imminent arrival and his subsequent arrest? Ten minutes perhaps? Fifteen at the most.

Urging himself onward until he was within a hundred feet from the Containment Wall, he hesitated, looking around to confirm he was still alone. He couldn't be the only one, surely? Why were there not others standing here, in this very same place and for the very same reason? The confusion inside his head having all but dispersed, he was able to view his situation with a restored sense of clarity. He'd been too long already and there could be no more delay. It was time to do what he'd come here to do. Reaching into his pocket, he withdrew a small electronic device, the size and shape of a pocket calculator, into which he tapped a seven digit code. Then, for the first time since being at school, he prayed out loud.

Holding the device in front of him like a gun, he slowly began to move forward, his body stooped and rigid like that of an advancing soldier. As angry bursts of energy snapped and danced before him, the fetid odour they released seemed almost to cling to his eyes. Undeterred, he continued to walk towards the wall, nearer and nearer, unable to look away as it snaked skywards, rippling and reflecting like the surface of a lake in a breeze. At only ten feet away, he pressed his thumb down firmly on the instrument's tiny control panel, immediately hearing the discord switch to another frequency—one which pulsated furiously back and forth. The change was dramatic, enabling an additional sound to cut through and add itself to the cacophony. This one came from above his head—the distinctive clatter of a helicopter's rotor blades.

As though receptive to his fear, the device had begun to tremble in his hand, rapidly becoming warm with the current which now flowed through it. Frantically he pressed it, over and over again, willing something—*anything*—to happen. Silently he counted the passing seconds . . .

And then, through dust-filled eyes, he watched as a fissure began to emerge in the wall before him, splitting open until something resembling a narrow passageway had formed. Irregular in shape and fluctuating in size, it was impossible to see through to the other side as he'd imagined he would be able to. A doorway to somewhere, or maybe nowhere—whatever; it made little difference to him anymore.

He took a final glance at the darkening skies above him and was gone.

1

Present day. 2057.

The north-east wind cut across the few remaining fields which surrounded Gunners Park, bringing with it little flurries of snow. Long-abandoned and now completely overgrown, many years had passed since this land yielded anything other than thistles and weeds. Only the decommissioned pylons remained, their galvanised skeletal frames seemingly impervious to the ravages of time. As landscapes go, it was as bleak as it was featureless, not a tree or hillock to break the acres of monotonous, grim nothingness.

In the distance, the stark silhouette of Mother City rose skyward, its cold and sepulchral presence dominating an otherwise empty horizon. Faceless grey buildings nestled amongst willowy, grey air-purification towers, a conglomeration of concrete monoliths, each one barely distinguishable from the other. Grey against yet more grey.

The coldest winter for nine years was still hanging on, reluctant to release its grip, its work as yet unfinished. It would be a little while longer before the next season would be ushered in.

Plumes of smoke spilled from chimney stacks and the blades of makeshift wind generators spun enthusiastically, their chattering the only sound to be heard except for the moaning of the wind.

On the driveway of a sizable, whitewashed property, an elderly man prodded and poked beneath the bonnet of an ancient pickup truck with an assortment of tools. Wearing a huge fur coat and leather cowboy-style hat, he would resurface from time to time to wipe his oil-covered hands on a piece of rag, and stare thoughtfully down at whatever it was that engrossed him. On the occasional trips he made to the driver's window, his movements were slow, and at times unsteady. Leaning in to crank the engine a few times, he would shake his head and mutter to himself as it coughed and died. So absorbed was he in his work that he failed to notice the impressively long and sleek black hover-car which had slowed down virtually to a standstill as it passed by, before swiftly accelerating away once more. Rounding the corner, it took a left turn into Gatling Drive, whereupon it headed towards its final destination, slowing down to skilfully negotiate a three-point turn immediately outside Number 7.

Number 7, a modest 'work in progress' bungalow, was the last but one house along, and probably the smallest. Built largely from cement block, it would never quite manage to lose its industrial image despite being topped with a corrugated tin roof painted in olive green. However, like many of the other converted dwellings on what had been until the millennium an industrial estate, it shared what some would describe as a 'rustic charm'. This was definitely not a sentiment shared by the passenger of the long, black machine which was now pulling up outside.

As the engine was shut off, the car sank slowly to the ground with a pneumatic hiss, and save for the ticking of hot metal beginning to cool, was silent. Along one of its highly-polished flanks, a door proceeded to open, sliding effortlessly towards the car's rear. No sooner had it come to rest, then a tall and rather elegant figure climbed out and walked towards the driver's window, stooping to rap on the glass with the handle of a walking cane. Only when the thin man seemed content that his instructions to the ferret-faced chauffeur had been fully understood, did he finally permit him to leave. His gaze followed the car as it lurched forward and sped away, before turning to look out across the barren fields to where the ghostly visage of the city loomed importantly, barely a couple of miles away. As always, he congratulated himself on his social standing within its walls, a great sense of pride swelling inside as he savoured the moment.

With a spring in his step, he made his way towards a front door that for as long as he could remember had been awaiting a top coat of paint to be applied to its dull cream primer. Set in a circular steel frame, a coloured glass window depicted a single pink rose, beneath which a small brass '7' was held in place by two screws. For reasons he'd never quite understood (and never been interested enough to ask about), this numeral had at some point in the past been repositioned upside down. As before, and the time before that, the thin man shook his head and frowned.

2

Inside the kitchen of Number 7 Gatling Drive, Marcus Calvert lay slumped across a time-yellowed, pine table, his head resting in the crook of his arm amongst an assortment of unfinished projects, books and amateur etchings. It was 9:30am and he'd risen only half an hour earlier, reluctantly dragging himself from his bed following what had been a typically short and broken night's sleep. He'd heaped an extra spoonful of coffee into his mug, but the caffeine had failed in its task; within ten minutes of sitting at the table, he was asleep.

Three sharp blows to his front door resonated like gunfire across the room, instantly jerking him back to reality as his midmorning daydream was brought to an untimely end. Lifting his head from the surrounding debris, he glanced towards a wooden carriage clock on the mantelpiece, and then towards the buff-coloured card propped up next to it. Holding a pair of wire-framed spectacles before his face, he rose gingerly from his chair and crossed the room to retrieve it. As he stood there absorbing its details, the date and time exquisitely penned in the familiar copper-coloured ink, his worst fears were confirmed. How could he have forgotten? It wasn't like he hadn't been given ample warning—a whole week in which to make sure he would be somewhere else when Hurst called. For a split second he contemplated sneaking to the back of the house and pretending he wasn't home—something he would have done (and had before, on more than one occasion) if he could be certain he hadn't already been spotted through the window.

Two more raps against the glass—*crack crack*—as though it was being struck with something hard. Calvert grimaced to himself. He'd missed his opportunity; the time for flight had passed. Still cursing his own carelessness, he grudgingly made his way to the door, mentally preparing himself for the lecture which he would no doubt be subjected to. The effects of the previous night's drinking had kicked in several hours earlier, refusing to be placated by anything from his medicine cabinet. Unusually for him, even the 'hair of the dog' remedy he normally swore by, was to prove just as useless. His stomach was still fragile, and despite having only just cleaned his teeth, his breath tasted foul.

Even on the occasions when he found himself *without* a hangover to contend with, Calvert could never raise even the slightest enthusiasm at the prospect of one of Hurst's visits. At best they could be described as tedious, and as far as he could ascertain, without any real purpose other than to remind him once again of his many failings. Thankfully, these impositions were few and relatively short.

Fumbling with the security chain and the stiff lock he'd been intending to free up for months, he pulled the door open, shivering as a blast of late February misery sneaked in around him.

'Good morning, Councillor,' he muttered, unaware of the slightly pained expression he was now wearing.

If it had been anyone other than the man who now stood before him, they would surely have picked up on the lack of conviction in this greeting—maybe even felt a little offended by it. Hurst, however, was by now not only long familiar with Calvert's reticence, but also seemingly immune to it. Either that or the passing years had gradually made him oblivious to such undertones.

'Marcus. Marcus. Sorry it's been such a while,' he gushed, breaking into a wide, toothy smile. Peering curiously at Calvert, his one uncovered eye was dark and shining—almost bird-like. 'You have remembered our appointment, I assume, yes?' As he spoke, Hurst repeatedly tapped the silver tip of a bespoke ebony cane against the concrete front step. Surmising that this latest fashion accessory had most likely been instrumental in the violation of his front door, Calvert chose to pay it no attention, let alone comment on it.

'Of course. Come in, Councillor,' he insisted, somewhat feebly, stepping aside to beckon his distinguished-looking caller into the warm chaos which served as both kitchen and dining room.

'Much obliged,' enthused Hurst, bowing his shaven head theatrically and brushing past Calvert in a somewhat grandiose manner. 'That wind cuts to the bone, does it not?'

'Yes, it sure does,' agreed Calvert, determined to keep his exchanges to the barest minimum in the hope that his visitor would say what he had to and leave him to suffer in peace.

The Councillor, however, did not seem to share the same desire to keep anything brief. The man was clearly in no hurry at all, floating randomly around the room, his long, thin hands clasped behind his back. Calvert watched with growing irritation as, for what seemed an unnecessary length of time, he then continued to study the small collection of faded family portraits grouped together above the mantelpiece, despite having seen them on numerous occasions.

With the appraisal finally completed, Hurst wandered over to the table. Here his attention was instantly drawn to the half-full tumbler of scotch, perched next to the entrails of some abandoned electronic gadget. 'Starting early these days, are we not, Marcus?' he chastised, tutting in his usual condescending manner, whilst raising the glass to his large and considerably hawkish nose.

Without bothering to reply, Calvert dropped down onto a battle-scarred leather chaise longue positioned in the darkest corner of the room. From here, he studied Hurst curiously. A chromium eye patch had replaced the usual black one, giving him something of a slightly android appearance, but apart from that, little else had changed. The knee-length black and blue leather coat—of which he was more than a little envious—was still belted tightly around his waist despite the warmth from the small, wood-burning stove. The gloves, as always, would remain on his hands. Calvert had never seen him without them.

Returning the tumbler back to its place amongst the clutter, Hurst looked up again, his face breaking into an apologetic smile. 'Sorry—not my business, I know,' he added with a dismissive gesture, before placing his bony backside on the corner of the table. Cupping his chin in his hand, he looked attentively at Calvert, and continued in a tone which was not so much sincere as patronising. 'But don't forget, I'm always here if there is anything you need to talk about—man to man, as they say.'

Reaching for his tobacco tin and flicking open the lid, Calvert shrugged indifferently, turning his attention to its contents. 'It's fine, it's just the one to help keep the cold out,' he lied, not in the least interested in either Hurst's opinions, or his offer of guidance. Despite believing the Councillor's concerns for his well-being to be genuine, the man's overbearing approach could at times be exhausting.

Placing a line of tobacco along the length of the cigarette paper, he proceeded to roll it expertly into a thin, neat tube between his fingers, before finishing it off with a single sweep of his tongue. Glancing up, he noticed the Councillor seemed to have become quite absorbed with one of the many dissected electronic projects lying on the table next to him.

'A Music Maid, if I'm not very much mistaken,' he proclaimed exuberantly, picking up a random piece of curved pink plastic to examine the image of the girl's face imprinted upon it, the open-mouthed smile no longer the revered and iconic trademark it once was. 'Now that certainly does take one back.'

Not for the first time, Calvert noticed Hurst had taken to dropping the pretentious 'one' into conversation, and smiled to himself. It would seem yet another affectation had been added to an already long list.

'Not seen one of these since, ah . . .' Hurst paused, nose pinched between finger and thumb for effect, screwing up his eyes in the process as if in pain from the depth of his concentration. 'Well, certainly not since the Dredge Wars.'

'It used to be Kim's—needs a new chip or something,' Calvert replied flatly, reaching for his lighter and firing the roll-up into life. 'It's been here for years. Just thought it might be interesting to see what songs are on it.'

'Hmm, quite.' Hurst seemed to have already lost interest in the Music Maid, now sliding his finger around a small control panel on the inside of his left wrist. 'Yes, an easy job for a man of your many talents, Marcus,' he continued, still making adjustments to the device. '*Wasted* talents, in my opinion.'

Here we go thought Calvert to himself, drawing deeply on his cigarette, holding it in his lungs for a few seconds before exhaling. He watched as the plume of blue smoke drifted lazily across the room, momentarily transfixed as it twisted and curled.

'This place really isn't good for your well-being, you know,' Hurst persisted, the sincere expression returning to his face once more. 'Isolation dampens a man's spirits—I'm sure of it.' Frowning, he waved an arm in front of his face in a melodramatic manner to emphasise his disdain for the nicotine cloud which had by now reached his nostrils. Rising from the edge of the table, he strode across the room to the window, where he proceeded to run a finger along the edge of the glass. 'Hmm . . . speaking of damp.' Peering out, he scanned the smooth pitch-black road that stretched past only about ten metres away. 'I take it you heard about Callingden?'

The hint of jubilation in Hurst's voice was not lost on Calvert.

'I did, yes, and it's bloody disgusting.'

Hurst spun round, glee written all over his face. 'Bloody old Darcey, you should have seen him. They actually dragged him kicking and screaming from his house in the end—silly old sod.'

By now well-accustomed to Hurst's opinions and warped sense of justice, Calvert took a deep breath, reminding himself once again to not be drawn in—to just let it go. But even as this thought passed through his head, he knew that for him, *just letting it go* was not an option. Without doubt, this would be the genuine reason for the Councillor's visit. The fall of Callingden was news he would have been unable to keep to himself for long.

Calvert, against his better judgement, took the bait. 'Personally, I admire the guy. He'd lived there for years and stuck to his guns. Why the hell should he move? As far as I'm concerned, *he* was in the right. It was his home, after all.'

'Poppycock!' exclaimed Hurst. 'He had ample opportunity to vacate the premises. The obstinate fool was given his papers to leave nearly six months ago. All the other tenants were agreeable with the alternative living arrangements offered to them.'

'I'm guessing they had little choice in the matter,' returned Calvert. 'I think it's sad. Callingden is a great little community.'

'*Was*, is more the operative word now, I think you'll find.' A lopsided smirk hovered for a few seconds, then vanished from Hurst's face. 'I passed it on my way over here, the bulldozers are clearing it as we speak.' He paused, switching back to his sincere tone. 'You know that *all* the non-metropolitan areas are required if the city is to expand, don't you, Marcus? This one included—it's only a question of time.'

'Don't!' Calvert raised both his hands up in front of him. 'I don't want to think about it.'

The Councillor shrugged, turning back to the window. 'Mother City, that's the only place to be these days. Higher standards of living—all the mod cons one could ever need. Sterilized food, purified air, you name it . . . ' He paused. 'It just makes sense.'

'Not to me, it doesn't. There's nothing there for me.'

'It's not healthy here anymore, Marcus, you know that. The air is toxic and getting worse by the day. You may not be able to notice it now, but give it a few more years and you will. At least in the city we have the purification towers to filter it. Where else in Sector 21 can offer that?'

Calvert didn't reply. He'd heard it all before—only about a month earlier.

Hurst continued to stare out through the small, misted-up panes. 'I can just about remember when this place used to be an industrial estate,' he declared absently. 'The Harper's place on the corner is actually part of what used to be a munitions factory before it got bombed. Mind you—it doesn't look much better these days, to be honest.' He then laughed at his own joke, conveniently forgetting he'd aired it on his last visit.

'Yeah, yeah, I know,' replied Calvert, choosing as before to ignore the wisecrack, 'and this house was Barnett's Auto Services. Gunners actually has some history attached to it—unlike your soulless city. For example, you see that concrete plinth out there? Well, that's where the petrol pumps used to be. Art told me a while back—reckons he can still remember them in use.'

'Quite,' replied the Councillor haughtily, turning and raising his one visible eyebrow. 'Not that it's wise to put *too* much faith in anything Arthur O'Sullivan has to say, but . . .' He shrugged, running a hand through his neat and very obviously dyed goatee. 'Then again, it's not really my business, but I just happen to believe the man has a few too many—how shall we put it—*issues*? Too much gone haywire up here, that's the problem.' He tapped the side of his forehead knowingly with his finger. 'How is the old renegade these days anyway? Still spouting his usual conspiracy claptrap?'

'Surely you know he's unwell?' Calvert found it impossible to believe Hurst would be unaware of Art's condition. 'As for his mind, he's still sharp as a razor.'

'Oh, come now, Marcus, listen to yourself. The man is totally delusional—has been for years. *And* a drug addict too, if the information I have recently received is correct—which I'm sure would be easy enough to verify.' The Councillor had now returned to

19

prodding at the electronic thing on his wrist. 'Where the hell is that idiot Deeks?'

Immediately his question was answered as an amused voice shrilled from the gadget. 'Idiot Deeks here at your service, Councillor Hurst.'

'You were supposed to have been here three minutes ago,' Hurst reprimanded, his embarrassment at having incorrectly set the functions plainly obvious.

Calvert, realising Deeks would have been listening in on their conversation, couldn't help but feel a little amused.

'On my way, sir,' quipped the voice. 'Oh, I nearly forgot—over and out.' A chuckle quickly followed, and then a click as connection was broken.

Turning back to the window, Hurst wiped away some condensation. 'You really need to set your sights a bit higher, Marcus; odd-jobbing is never going to make you a wealthy man.' As if to add emphasis to his words, he pointed outside at nothing in particular. 'It's an exciting new world out there, you know—one that's filled with opportunity. Do you not wish to be part of it?'

'Not really,' returned Calvert, relighting the roll-up. 'For one thing, I actually like my work, however lowly you might consider it; and for another, I happen to find much of this so-called "exciting new world" filled with superficial and rather dull people. Sorry, but from where I'm sitting it all just looks a little false.'

'*False*, you say?' Hurst turned, his face a mask of disbelief. 'If that is indeed the case, then ask yourself why so many out there choose to welcome it? It's a fact, the population is more content today than they have ever been.'

'You mean more *deluded* than they've ever been.'

'Nonsense, Marcus, absolute nonsense. If you were to take the trouble to look at the government statistics, you would find yourself to be somewhat in the minority.' Hurst lifted the eyebrow again. 'You can't stop change, you know—it's inevitable.'

'Who said anything about stopping it? I'm just not prepared to get swept up in it like everyone else feels the need to.' Calvert wished the Councillor would just leave.

'Take your father, for example,' Hurst droned on. 'Now there was a man who understood the necessity to constantly push things forward, to . . . *evolve*. Yes, that's what it's all about—evolving. Without that zeal, the human race would still be in caves, rubbing sticks together to make fire and communicating in monosyllabic grunts. Suffice to say, the world as we know it today would be a sorry place, if not for man's desire to advance. It's what defines us as a species, after all.'

'But at what cost?' cried Calvert, annoyed with himself at being drawn into a debate he had little chance of winning. 'Even if society has to suffer as a result?'

'You've not read the philosophies of the late Sir Isaac Bartock, I presume, Marcus?'

'No, I haven't,' conceded Calvert, beginning to tire of Hurst's patronising tone and inferences.

The Councillor nodded. 'I suspected as much—it's quite serious stuff, definitely not for everyone . . . but I will attempt to encapsulate his ideology as best I can.' Here he paused for effect before continuing. 'Bartock believed it was the fundamental duty of every man in a position of influence to leave his mark upon the world, in whichever way he felt compelled to do so, without constraint or the threat of recrimination. In other words, these torchbearers should not be held back by the fear of crossing lines that others with less imagination might deem unethical, or at times, even unlawful. Sometimes these boundaries *have* to get pushed aside in the pursuit of enlightenment and progression. So, on such occasions when this might occur, the *sin*' (here, Hurst added some finger quotes for emphasis) 'has to be considered an insignificant sacrifice towards the greater good—therefore, lawful . . . unlike certain crimes and debacles committed through ignorance and apathy.'

All too often in the past, Calvert had been unwillingly subjected to the Councillor's enthusiastic and—in his opinion, rather questionable views regarding such matters as power structures and eugenics. Now apparent that once again he'd taken his eye off the ball, only to become the recipient of an all too familiar sermon, he cursed his own lack of attentiveness. Albeit unintentionally, he had flicked a switch—one which past experience should have taught him to leave well alone. But, however suffocating the man's presence might be, Calvert was, as usual, too stubborn to back down. 'And what a cold, corruptible world that would be, certainly not a—'

'Look,' Hurst interrupted, 'I'm not implying that virtues such as compassion and understanding, etcetera, have no relevance in these times—of course not.' A serious expression now clouded his face. 'Only that maybe they can, on occasion, obscure the bigger picture.'

'Which is?'

Hurst hesitated, moving away from the window. 'Optimisation of the species, I suppose . . . survival of the fittest.' He held up his hand to silence Calvert, whose mouth had just fallen open. 'Do you really think we would have come this far if men such as Darwin and Newton had chosen to abandon science to, let's say, care for the elderly or knit blankets for stray cats? No, Marcus, that's not how it works at all. The world is the amazing place it is for no other reason than because great men have shaped it this way, nothing more.'

'You don't ever feel we've gone too far? That we should maybe rewind a little?' questioned Calvert, beginning to feel he might have lost the debate and almost past caring.

'Are you serious? Look at our achievements in just the last thirty years. Before that, we had children killing each other on the streets—poverty and homelessness out of control, plus the continual threat of global terrorism to contend with on a daily basis. All that has now gone.' Hurst swept his hand sideways in a slicing motion, his voice rising. 'Eliminated—relegated to the history books.'

'But it's only the constant fear of the satellites that keeps everyone in line, not morality or respect.'

'And what of it? Even if that were the case—which I certainly do not believe it to be—does it matter? *How* it is controlled is not the issue, simply that it *is*. Tell me, can you see these satellites?'

'No, of course not,' replied Calvert, 'but I still know they're there, watching me.'

'Ah yes, but only because you have been *told* so,' countered Hurst. 'Do you have anything to hide? No—so why then should it bother you? Only the guilty amongst us have anything to fear from them. Think about it, it's not like they are hovering a couple of feet above your house, blocking out the sunlight, is it? They are so far away, they're not even detectable—let alone be considered a possible impingement upon your privacy.' He raised a gloved finger before his face, his tone becoming ever more condescending as he continued. 'Remember, Marcus, our technology works for us . . .' Here again, he paused for effect, '*Not* against us.' Hurst finished this statement off with a flourish, obviously pleased with it. So theatrical was his delivery, Calvert almost expected him to take a bow. Instead, he just checked the device on his wrist, tapping it irritably. 'Where the hell has Deeks got to? The bloody man should have been here ages ago.'

Truth be known, Councillor Hurst would have happily dispensed with Oswald Deeks' services pretty soon after taking him into his employment, but for one reason alone. Quite simply, he was the best hover-car driver available, and these days they happened to be in short supply. Be that as it may, he'd been getting a little too cocky lately, and needed bringing down a peg or two.

Just as he turned back to the window, the recently purchased GlydeMaster pulled up outside, the soft burble of its hydrogen-powered engine barely audible through the glass. The same could not be said for the inharmonious dirge coming from the onboard sound system. As the rear door opened, it now spewed out into the cold air, shattering the peace and tranquility of Gatling Drive, its aggressive thumping as unmelodic and repetitive as any factory machinery.

'Damn that idiot,' cursed Hurst, striding outside and making haste to the driver side window to take his displeasure out on the small and rather shifty-looking creature sat inside. The furious music snapped off instantly, leaving just the pleasing murmur from the long chromium exhausts which ran along each side of the shiny black paintwork.

Calvert followed, shoulders hunched against the cold, to give the GlydeMaster the obligatory once over. Hovering lazily just a couple of inches above the tarmac, it gleamed in the weak sunlight, rocking under its own latent power. He nodded in the general direction of Deeks, but the driver seemed too preoccupied with the bollocking he was currently receiving to notice. Running his eyes over the bodywork, he was forced to admit it was a very impressive-looking machine, no doubt about it—unquestionable craftsmanship and style.

Having finished with Deeks, Hurst swaggered over to join him. 'Gorgeous, isn't she?' he bragged, stroking the elegantly curved roof. 'It's the latest model—only just been launched. The *Saturn Plus.* As you can probably tell, it's top of the range. Rather expensive at eighty-five thousand denarii . . . but then, you get what you pay for, don't you? Quality doesn't come cheap, as they say.'

'True.' Calvert nodded, not wishing to engage in any conversation likely to further inflate the Councillor's already oversized ego. 'Hover-cars don't really do it for me though, not my thing.'

'Really?' exclaimed Hurst, looking at him with an over-exaggerated expression of bewilderment. 'You don't know what you're missing. But seriously, Marcus, think about what I have said. Mother City is where it's all happening these days. It's not healthy being stuck out here in the back of beyond—look what it's done to O'Sullivan.' And with a small bow of his head, he climbed into the back of the waiting car. After barking some instructions at Deeks, the door then closed smoothly behind him with little more than a gentle hum. A tinted window slid down to reveal the Councillor cocooned in palatial splendour. 'Think about it, Marcus. This place is—to put it kindly—a little below par, and quite frankly, you deserve better. Let me find you a nice apartment, well inside the Inner Zones—all the mod cons you could think of. Twenty-four hour surveillance systems, air towers, built-in mood analysers—the lot. As I said before, it makes sense.' And then, with a circular wave of the hand followed by '*au revoir*, Marcus,' the GlydeMaster Saturn Plus rose up on its haunches, pushing a welcoming blast of warm air towards Calvert's feet in the process. Within seconds it was out of sight, leaving him just standing there, asking himself 'did he really just say *au revoir*?'

Back inside, he picked up the whisky tumbler, swallowing its contents in one. Convincing himself that a refill was well-deserved, he reluctantly made it a small one. Sitting back down at the table, he smiled to himself. *Built-in mood analysers?* He'd never heard of anything so stupid. However, the smile quickly faded as he noticed a recent addition to the usual clutter upon his table. In his haste, Councillor Hurst had left behind the chic ebony and silver walking cane; any day now, he would very likely be returning to claim it.

3

Gideon Hurst was restless. Even the snifter of his excellent cognac was doing little to appease the dour mood that had fallen upon him. A Brahms violin concerto floated from walnut-encased speakers, positioned high on the wall above the white patent leather couch on which he now reclined, staring up at the ceiling.

The state-of-the-art music player was one of his most prized possessions—in fact, the room was practically designed around its existence. Many hours had been consumed researching its optimal placement, diligent attention paid to what he liked to refer to as its 'sweet spot'.

'*This* is it,' he'd once declared to a totally disinterested Deeks, whilst standing in the middle of the room with his arms spread like some crucified effigy of Jesus Christ, the latest jazz fusion tracks blasting out from the newly-acquired Audio Tsar IV. 'Here, just here—can't you feel it? *This* is the exact point where the waveforms meet.' He had then proceeded to share his extensive knowledge of its inner qualities and technical specifications, before reaching the conclusion that he was only wasting his breath on the likes of Oswald Deeks. Damn it, why did the man irritate him so much?

On their journey home from the visit with Marcus, Deeks had repeatedly glanced over his left shoulder, attempting to engage him in some puerile conversation in that annoying 'cheeky chappie' manner of his. Something about a new pleasure bar opening up immediately opposite his apartment, how expensive it was—but well worth it just for the women alone. He'd then had the gall to flash Hurst a leery smile in the rear view mirror. The Councillor hadn't been in the slightest bit interested, and as good as told him so, before reprimanding him on the matter of his tardiness and rather dishevelled appearance of late.

His meetings with Marcus Calvert often left him feeling a little subdued, and today was no exception. Something about his negative outlook and tunnel-visioned beliefs never failed to frustrate him. Surely he couldn't really be satisfied with simply muddling along while the world passed by outside his door? It was unnatural for a man to not wish to achieve. Then again, he'd never been any different. Even as a child, Marcus had been a little withdrawn, never one to push himself—not like some of the precocious offspring his colleagues would go on to produce.

As the son of his friend and one-time business partner Valentine, Marcus had been the only infant who Hurst ever really formed any kind of bond with. On his visits to the Calvert family home, he'd even taken to referring to himself as Uncle Gideon in the boy's presence in the hope that the name might stick. However, it would soon become embarrassingly obvious that it was never going to take, and he'd eventually given up and dropped it.

When Valentine disappeared some years later—never to resurface, Hurst had secretly hoped that he himself might be called upon to pick up the gauntlet and take on the role as some kind of mentor to the boy. Sadly, this wasn't to be, and the young Marcus Calvert instead gravitated towards long-time family friend Arthur O'Sullivan who lived on the Gunners Park estate, only a stone's throw away from where Marcus himself now resided.

Hurst held little fondness for O'Sullivan, and was never truly comfortable around him. Something about his presence unnerved him, and had done for as long as he could remember. Despite it being close to thirty years ago, he still harboured a resentment that Valentine had seen fit to invite him into the inner sanctum of the AIR-Group company at all. Worse still, the recruitment of a man who Hurst would rapidly come to regard as something of a radical was undertaken without his prior agreement—or even his knowledge.

He'd known from the word go that O'Sullivan was never going to fit in at the AIR-Group (Advanced Intelligence Research). From his nonchalant attitude and weird sense of humour, it hadn't been difficult to detect that he was one of life's misfits. Although much time had passed since then, there was still little change in Hurst's feelings towards him. He was also of the opinion that the man's anti-government stance and somewhat anarchic views could only have been a negative influence on the young Calvert in his impressionable formative years. Nothing in his own psyche would ever allow him, even for one minute, to consider the possibility that his bitterness towards him might possibly be motivated by nothing more than jealousy.

Hurst had never really wanted children of his own, and his lack of desire or effort to engage with women throughout his life would ensure that fatherhood was unlikely to happen. Not that he was homosexual or odd in any way; he'd just never been interested in anything that might distract him from his work. Like all young men, in his youth he'd consorted with girls—gone through the requisite motions and the obligatory bragging in the bars afterwards as would have been expected, but deep down inside he knew it just wasn't for him. Now at the age of seventy-one, it still wasn't, but Hurst was very aware of a hollowness which lurked somewhere deep within him, a void that seemed only to grow with each passing year.

'Decrease volume ten percent,' he instructed the AutoButler as he rose from the couch. 'And while you're at it, another cognac.'

'Very good, sir,' replied a mechanical but very convincing Winston Churchill voice from behind a steel grating in the ceiling. Instantly, Brahms dropped in volume, and within seconds the liqueur appeared, sliding through a hatch in the wall before coming to rest on a small silver tray. Reaching for it, Hurst then began to pace backwards and forwards across the room, the crystal snifter pressed to his forehead as though its cool touch might bring some clarity to his thoughts. Casting his mind back to the morning's conversation, he tried to recall everything he'd said. Had he allowed himself to become sidetracked? Possibly—but at times it could be frustrating trying to get through to Marcus, who constantly found it necessary to reject any form of level-headed ideology. He didn't think he'd handled it badly, but maybe, on second thoughts, his comments regarding Arthur O'Sullivan's recently discovered drug addiction might have been unwise. He was also very aware that he hadn't properly addressed a particular subject—one that had been the very reason for his visit.

'Mute sound one hundred percent and reduce lighting thirty,' he demanded, removing the chromium eye patch and walking to a corner of the room to ease himself into what he'd come to think of as his 'pleasure chair'.

'Very good, sir,' replied the Churchillian voice of the AutoButler, as it set about fine-tuning the ambience to its master's requirements.

After stripping off his clothes, Hurst then proceeded to make himself comfortable in the chair, before reaching for a strange-looking piece of apparatus which was hooked over one of its arms. This he now positioned on his head, before making a couple of adjustments to a cluster of controls located on its right hand side.

The headpiece consisted of what appeared to be a grey metal skull cap, from which a thin loom of various coloured wires protruded. These in turn fed into a dark blue visor strip about two inches wide, running from ear to ear and completely covering his eyes. From there, more wires ran to a rather crude-looking control box, fixed to a stand and positioned within arms' reach of where he now sat, eagerly fingering the dials on its luminous front panel. This was Hurst's one guilty pleasure, and truth be known, had become something of his *raison d'etre* over the recent months.

Despite successfully convincing himself that the matter was firmly in hand, and that it would be used only in strict moderation, the allure of the headpiece was proving difficult to resist. Deep down he knew he had something of a problem; however, an unshakeable confidence in his own self-resilience would never allow this suspicion to be given any serious consideration. For him, there was never a moment's doubt that when the time came, he would be able to just walk away without so much as looking back over his shoulder. Unfortunately, the reality of the matter was that he'd become every bit as enslaved by his own personal addiction as any of the city's hordes of street corner junkies with their Opioid Oblivion fixes and vacant expressions.

Be that as it may, narcotics played no part in the desires of Gideon Hurst. His compulsion was for his own creation, the prototype Vortex Subcon MK-2—known simply as the VS-2.

4

With a mumble, the shuttle pulled into its designated dropping off place, gently releasing a tide of air before lowering itself to greet the tarmac. A couple of seconds later, audio instructions from the automated driver were transmitted to the two passengers presently waiting to dismount. From the remote cab at the front of the vehicle, its synthetic voice crackled through the onboard sound system. 'Destination complete. Commuters please dismount. We *do* hope you have a pleasant evening.' All delivered with irritatingly over-sincere enunciation.

The journey into the city centre had been a non-eventful twenty minute ride, the hover-shuttle efficiently dealing with any traffic situations which arose en route. The only other passenger was a young woman, probably no older than Calvert's own son. For the entire journey, she'd stood there looking miserable—statue-still, with a small white hand wrapped around the steel handrail. Like most of the younger generation these days, her face was partly obscured by the fashionable X-Specs lenses, now glowing incandescently, turning her pale skin an even paler shade of blue. Ridiculously underdressed in a short red skirt which barely covered her behind, and a skimpy jacket failing to reach her bare midriff, she shivered in the sub-zero conditions. Calvert had smiled at her in a friendly and (what he hoped was) a reassuring manner when she first boarded; either she didn't notice, or she'd simply chosen not to engage.

Stepping down from the shuttle's footplate, the cold air hit him, and not for the first time since setting out earlier, he found himself questioning his reasons for leaving the warmth of his stove. Resisting the temptation to climb back on and head home again, he instead thrust his hands as deeply into his jacket pockets as he could, before heading off in the direction of what was regarded to be the hub of the city's nightlife.

As he drew nearer, mechanical music spilled out from the taverns and bars—boomy and frenetic, as it raced along the side streets towards him. Beneath his feet, heat from the underground pipes seeped upwards through the pavement, finding its way into his chilled bones—one feature of the Inner Zones which even he was forced to admit was pleasing. Looking around him, he was surprised by how much had changed. Every third or fourth building now seemed to be one of these new pleasure bars Elliot had mentioned when they last met. To Calvert, only now seeing them for the first time, their presence seemed somewhat uninviting and more than a little intimidating. Outside their gaping doorways, huge, dark-suited brutes stood sentry—motionless in their wide leg power stances, their 'don't fuck with me' expressions partially concealed behind dark glasses.

Far above his head, mobile searchlights roamed the sky, throwing down beams of invasive, harsh white light as they transmitted messages to the scout cameras below. On top of steel posts, these now rotated back and forth, diligently scrutinising humanity as it moved around them. Calvert watched the faces of two young women, momentarily lit up by the glare, seemingly unconcerned that their entire history would, without doubt, have just been screened. Everything—who they were, where they had just been, who they had last slept with—all added to some hideous government data bank. Here it would be stored away for possible use against them, if deemed necessary at some future date. Immorally obtained ammunition, with little fear of return fire.

Calvert found himself wondering how extensive the file on himself would be, and whether he was already classified as a person of interest by the Directorate of Law and Order. Having always considered himself something of a nobody, the possibility of this both intrigued and amused him somewhat. Maybe that could be his epitaph? He pictured it in gold lettering, carved into a black granite headstone.

HERE LIES A PERSON OF INTEREST
SOMEONE WHO NEVER QUITE FITTED IN

Yeah, that would work.

Making his way down Saviour Street, he saw little he recognised from his past, and even less that gave him hope for the future. Unable to see these pleasure bars as anything other than modern day enslavement, Calvert could not understand their allure, instantly dismissing them as yet another example of corporate parasites cashing in on a weak-minded populace. How easy it was to simply distract and exploit them with gadgetry and sedentary pleasures, all in the guise of entertainment. Surely he couldn't be alone in this belief—there must be others who see it too? In his mind's eye, he could almost picture it like some malicious life form crawling around him, cackling maniacally as it crept from street to street, sucking dry a once-beautiful city of its very heart and soul. Everywhere he looked, the bars seemed to have commandeered the Inner Zones, their modern chic image a stark contrast to the abandoned buildings which surrounded them. To Calvert, now eyeing these empty lifeless shells, it seemed almost impossible to believe that not so long ago they had been thriving businesses, with people actually working alongside each other; talking, laughing—*communicating* with each other, in ways which would be seen as odd nowadays.

Today they stood as little more than silhouettes in the gloom, like decaying teeth soon to be removed, forlorn and forgotten; crumbling red brickwork beneath rotting wooden fascia. Eventually, when his own generation moved on, so they too would cease to exist—even as a memory.

He stopped outside The Prism, the one venue which, according to Kim, was a frequent haunt of Elliot's. Stepping up to the window, he cupped his hands around his face in an attempt to peer in, but found himself unable to do so due to the impenetrable blackness of the glass. As he tried again—this time from a different angle, a humming sound from just above his head startled him, causing him to back away. A large and rather unwieldy-looking camera was swivelling around on its mounting, coming to rest with its long black lens pointing in his direction. Various coloured lights now lit up as it whirred noisily in and out, adjusting its focus to examine him.

Calvert immediately relaxed, relieved to see it was nothing more than a standard old-school type security camera. These he had no issues with—unlike the government-controlled 'Snoopers' which patrolled the city in large numbers as they carried out their business of collecting information. Virtually silent, these machines could be seen (or often not) either sneaking around the streets or discreetly skulking in the shadows, their lightweight alloy and carbon fibre bodies hovering a mere few inches above the ground. Never off duty, their mission was a simple one: *Observe—Collect—Report*. Everything documented—nothing omitted. Their relentless twenty-four hour surveillance programme would ensure that crime was kept to an all-time low. Yet despite this, to Calvert, their presence was both intrusive and unsettling. In his eyes, a Snooper was an automated abomination—the devil itself, enclosed in a metal shell. He'd come to loathe them with a passion, even more so than the stationary scout cameras, along with everything else they represented.

Deceptively introduced to the population sometime after the Dredge Wars of 2026 as Mobile Security Officers (or M.S.O.s), their official role was stated to be that of city guardians. In Calvert's belief, the truth was something far more sinister: their very existence constituted a violation of privacy. In the same manner that the overused and rather transparent 'all done in the interest of national security' excuse could be used to legitimise any violation against a person's liberties, so too could the 'our public's safety is paramount' mantra. At any given opportunity, either of these terminologies could be applied to a situation, and the 'necessary action' taken. The form this action would generally take was the immediate dispatching of a mob of Snoopers to the address of anyone considered an *undesirable,* with the sole purpose of intimidation. To complain would be tantamount to an admission of guilt, only inviting suspicion, which would inevitably lead to even higher levels of surveillance being carried out over a prolonged period. Strangely to Calvert, a large number of the city's inhabitants actually believed the official narrative where the M.S.O.s were concerned, and seemed almost relaxed around them. Not so for the majority of Gunners Park residents, who regarded all Snoopers with fear and distrust—especially Art O'Sullivan, whose hatred for them bordered on the pathological.

In appearance, they were little more than a convex disc of about four feet in diameter, from the centre of which arose a vertical tube-like apparatus. This was both flexible and telescopic, enabling it not only the ability to twist and turn in any direction, but also to extend itself to great heights. Capped with a revolving, globular head where the arm-like appendage that housed the camera eye was fixed, the loathsome thing was permitted a three hundred and sixty degree viewpoint of anything (and more to the point, any*one*) around it.

Calvert had once been told by Art that the optic beam within the camera section was so powerful, it was able to penetrate through eighteen inches of concrete with little trouble. Also—again according to Art—one night about ten years ago, immediately following a drinking session, he and a friend stumbled upon one broken down on the edge of Gunners Park. Apparently, the friend had sneaked back

35

there later on with a can of petrol, doused it and set it alight. Calvert was never quite sure if the story was true, but he liked to think it was.

Despite assurances from official sources that the Snoopers were non-aggressive in their pursuit of policing Sector 21, he'd recently discovered this claim to be untrue. About two months ago, a rumour had first begun to circulate; one which spoke of Gunners Park resident, Imogen Harper being attacked by an M.S.O. whilst returning home at dusk. Apparently she'd been knocked to the ground by some kind of high energy electrical current—or so he'd been informed by his next door neighbour a couple of days after the incident was said to have taken place. Although many at the time refused to believe the tale, Calvert was left in little doubt as to its authenticity, and had since—on the rare occasions when he was to encounter a Snooper—chosen to give it an even wider berth than before.

Now observing The Prism, his initial impression was that it seemed a little understated, at least compared to some of the other pleasure bars he'd just passed. Where was the tacky laser light display, or the requisite, heavy-duty neanderthal duo in their shades and suits? Lacking the ostentatiousness that seemed to accompany the larger, more corporate venues, there was almost an antiquated charm and friendliness to it. Momentarily he considered going in—even had his hand on the door, before common sense prevailed. What the hell was he thinking? Shaking his head, as if to rid himself of this ill-timed rush of impulsiveness, he turned and hurried away, suddenly anxious to put some distance between himself and The Prism. Even if Elliot was in there, what would be his reaction to him suddenly turning up unannounced, having not seen him for months? No, it would have been awkward for both of them—a ridiculous and uncharacteristically rash idea, which thankfully he'd had the sense to abort.

Crossing the road, still berating himself, he failed to notice the solitary Snooper, inconspicuously hovering above a small patch of waste ground to his left. Swaying gently from side to side, its dull grey form reflected no light at all, rendering it virtually invisible against the

36

derelict concrete murkiness behind. So lost was Calvert in his thoughts that he was oblivious to the red eye now watching him attentively, until finally, he dropped from its line of vision.

Rounding the corner, he was relieved to see his old haunt, The Marionette, still standing. Furthermore, despite years of obvious neglect, it was pretty much as he remembered it. Above him, the same old metal sign still hung from the barge boards, swinging back and forth in the wind, the painted dancing jester now all but faded from existence.

How long had it been since he'd last crossed its threshold? Twenty years? Maybe even closer to twenty-five. Not since Elliot had been born, *that* he was certain of. For a moment he just stood there, transfixed as long-forgotten memories rolled around his head like an old cinematic film reel—some good, others not so great.

Pushing open the heavy, glass-panelled door, he wandered into the shabby front hallway, soaking up the nostalgia as his eyes rediscovered the green, fern-patterned paper which was still just about clinging to the walls. From here, two doors offered the option of left for saloon, or right for bar. Calvert smiled, remembering the same old line he predictably would have used standing in this exact spot with Kim all those years ago. 'We must be barristers . . . as I'm getting called to the bar,' he whispered to himself, pushing open the door to the latter and tentatively making his way across the uneven, dark-stained floorboards.

Seated behind a trio of grubby-looking beer pumps, the bottle-blonde, mustachioed bartender barely lifted his eyes from the handheld gadget he was currently prodding. Calvert, recognising ignorance when he saw it, wasted no time on pleasantries or small talk. 'Bourbon and black—no ice,' he instructed tersely, not surprised in the slightest when little more than a grunt was offered in return. Reluctantly the bartender stopped playing with whatever it was in his hand, and gracelessly slewed himself off his seat to slump over to the optics, making little attempt to conceal a yawn as he did so.

Watching him with some amusement, Calvert pulled a rather bedraggled ten denarii note from his pocket, not even certain they would accept it. Deliberately placing it in a puddle of spilt beer which he reasoned to himself should have been wiped up, he then hauled himself up onto the only stool provided.

On his return the bartender snatched the note up, holding it to the light above his head for inspection. A look of irritation—or maybe suspicion—crossed his face, before eventually he seemed satisfied enough with whatever it was he was looking for. Skulking off to the till, he then proceeded to rummage around in it, eventually returning to the bar to plonk a couple of coins down in the same pool of spilt beer which, seconds ago, he'd retrieved the note from. Raising his eyes to meet Calvert's, he allowed a petty smirk to cross his face before reacquainting himself with his seat and electronic device. He'd successfully managed the whole exchange without so much as a word.

'*Touché*,' muttered Calvert under his breath, turning slowly and scanning the room.

Sadly, any charm and vibrancy The Marionette might have once possessed appeared to have long since left the building, along with its clientele. Apart from an elderly, rather haggard-looking character in the corner and two skinny youths equipped with those blue lenses that seemed to be all the rage, he was alone.

The old guy was seated at a small table with a half-pint glass of dark beer in front of him, as yet untouched. Bowed low over the newspaper he was reading, he swayed slightly from side to side as if in the process of nodding off. His face was deeply creased with that sallow complexion which comes only from a lifetime of heavy smoking. Partially obscured by his paper, and precariously close to the edge of the table, sat a large glass ashtray where a cigarette was smouldering away. Without once averting his eyes from the print before him, the old man would grab at it with a claw-like hand and draw deeply until it glowed like a hot coal. It was the same when returning it, his gaze remained permanently fixed to the newspaper. After each cigarette was stubbed out, he would light another before reaching into his pocket to throw what looked to be a small chunk of meat to a scrawny, rather moth-eaten mongrel lying by his feet. There was definitely a pattern to it—possibly even ritualistic by now. *Grab—inhale—return—grab—inhale—return—grab—inhale—return —stub out—replace—feed dog . . . repeat ad infinitum . . .*

Twisting himself around on his stool, Calvert turned his attention to the two young men on the opposite side of the room. Both were painfully thin, their faces decked out with various metalwork beneath identical close-cropped hairstyles. In fact, so similar was their appearance to each other, he wondered if they might be brothers. They were sitting about a foot apart on one of two long wooden benches which ran along the length of the wall, their heads tilted back against the nicotine-stained wall behind them. Despite their proximity, neither looked or spoke to the other, as if they were unaware of anyone else's presence—maybe even their own. Their eyes revealed nothing, all but hidden from view behind the flickering lenses, their faces illuminated by opalescent blue light. Transfixed, they stared straight ahead, their only movements being to periodically reach down to the low table in front of them and sip at disgusting-looking, milky-grey drinks through ridiculously long, bendy straws.

Just what it was they were tuned into that was so all-consuming, Calvert couldn't imagine, but it was obviously something more stimulating than the gloom this place had to offer. So why weren't they in the pleasure bars along with the rest of the younger generation? Then again, how long would it be until this place became one also? Not much longer, he suspected, especially if this evening's trade was a true reflection of business.

He'd never been inside a pleasure bar—or even worn a pair of X-Specs glasses for that matter, and was unlikely to do either. The whole concept of them was as alien to him as anything he could possibly imagine, only serving to highlight all that was so wrong in an ever-dividing society. Maybe Art was right; perhaps the only effective method of maintaining law and order was to keep people apart. It was certainly true that together they possessed the strength to overturn the system. Whether they would ever actually use it—that was another matter entirely.

Suddenly his mind was transported back thirty-five years or more. Once again he was a child, sitting in the cinema next to his mother, clutching an oversize box of popcorn, excited by the tiered seating and the massive images on the screen. All around him, people were sitting together, lifting hands to mouths as they whispered to each other, enjoying not just the film, but also the sharing of it. Now, sitting here more than three decades later, he realised he could actually recall the film with surprising clarity, despite at the time not having been quite able to understand the plot.

The Old River King—a romantic tale about the captain of an old paddle steamer—had been his mother's choice, and as was often the case, another family treat his father failed to put in an appearance for. How strange that after all these years of not thinking about it at all, to be suddenly reminded of a movie he'd not even particularly enjoyed. Obviously something must have triggered it, but for the life of him he couldn't imagine what it might be.

Long ago, in his mind he'd constructed what he would come to think of as *no-fly zones*—places he refused to let his thoughts stray to. Although an effective mechanism for keeping out unwanted nihilism and negativity, this was not a perfect solution; the main problem being that the walls he'd mentally installed to protect himself from his own darkness also held back many other things as well. Despite what Calvert had come to view as a predominantly shitty childhood, there were, in fact, many happy experiences he'd unintentionally all but erased from his own memory.

Like many other social pursuits, the cinemas and theatres were closed down during the Dredge Wars, with assurances they would be reopened once world peace was restored. They hadn't been, and just like they did with everything else, people soon got over it.

But the public was not to be left wanting for entertainment, the void would soon be filled. As flesh and blood social interaction died, a new ideology was given birth to—one which would be fervently fed by the ambitions of moguls, and the greed of magnates. Over a surprisingly short period of time, these *robber barons* successfully managed to steer society towards more reclusive pursuits, and for most, company would be in the form of whatever electronic gadgetry happened to be currently trending. Now they had the booths, of course, and for the younger generation especially, these were pretty much a way of life.

Calvert could clearly remember the first time he'd seen the adverts for them, and his feelings of despair at knowing their arrival in the city to be imminent. Rows and rows of the miserable things, utilitary in design, solitary in purpose, proudly displayed on every billboard. 'COMPLETE ISOLATION GUARANTEED' boasted the headings. 'YOUR PRIVACY IS PARAMOUNT' ran the jargon. Calvert suspected the first statement might have some truth to it, but doubted any credibility they might wish to attach to the second.

Gradually over the last decade, these highly addictive pleasure bars with their pleasure booths (why did everything now need to contain the word 'pleasure' when it clearly wasn't so?) had all but taken over the traditional bars and taverns. To his dismay, their encroachment onto the high streets would typically be met with very little opposition. This was mainly due to coercion and intimidation from those with a financial interest in their success, but also there seemed to be a general reluctance from people to challenge *anything*. It was less hassle to either just look away or simply fall in line. What was happening to social interaction—the desire to communicate face to face with another human being? Had it really been nothing more than a passing phase? How was it possible to simply cast it aside as one would an item of clothing that was now unfashionable or no longer fitted?

The thought that society could be so fickle was one which greatly depressed Calvert. As a younger man he'd been quite the social type—not a party animal by any means, but part of a group who would regularly meet up to drink and immerse themselves in conversation. Why did such behaviour need to be confined to the past, like some strange medieval practice one might read about in a long-forgotten history book?

Taking a mouthful of the sweet bourbon, he closed his eyes as he felt it hit the spot, wishing he'd thought to order a large one instead of a single. How had it all gone so wrong? How could even the most ignorant of the masses have been duped into believing that anything produced in the last thirty years was even remotely beneficial to them? He tried to pinpoint when the first signs of deterioration would have shown themselves, and whether the decline was a gradual one, or as Art believed, a direct result of the Dredge Wars.

Being only twelve years of age when the war came about, he'd not been particularly interested in what was happening around him politically—he certainly had no awareness as to possible future implications. Like many other kids of his generation, he'd felt almost traumatised by the shutdown of the internet, having never known a world without it. He could still remember the bitter resentment which, at times, felt as though it would consume him—the overwhelming sense of loss and injustice. A huge part of his life had just been ripped away, stolen from him; a future without it could only be a bleak one. As it turned out, adapting to the new *post-internet* world wasn't as grim as he'd imagined it would be. He certainly hadn't struggled long-term to function without it.

Art O'Sullivan was convinced the population had been deceived regarding the official explanation for its demise, and the genuine reason for the internet's removal was down to it offering people too much freedom of expression. His theory (of which there were many) was the more you permitted the masses to publicly voice their opinions, then obviously the more likely they would be to draw out others who shared them also. This wasn't a problem while the population were sharing holiday pics, first days at school pics and whatever pets happened to be around pics, but then the subject matter had changed. A small group of people were beginning to question the 'facts' reported by the government-controlled media platforms, not really in great enough numbers to do the establishment any real damage, but the underlying threat was enough to cause them some degree of unease. For the first time ever, seeds of doubt had been sown and the mainstream narrative on certain delicate subjects was being questioned. Rumours once confined only to the corridors of power now began to raise their ugly—and often perverted—heads on a global stage. Resignations in high places followed, and a few sacrificial lambs in lower ones were slaughtered to appease those who unquestioningly clung to the belief that democracy still lived, and that justice would always prevail.

But 'lessons had been learned.' Not moral ones—there would be little change there. No, what had become clearly evident was that, for a select few to continue to indulge in certain 'pleasures,' their behaviour would need to be kept strictly *under the radar.* And so, the solution was to raise levels of censorship to heights never previously witnessed, and pretend the problem had been dealt with.

Yet it still would not be enough to satisfy the guilty. Despite the success of hastily implemented government subterfuge, those who controlled the gatekeepers had been left feeling a little anxious. However vigilant their methods of monitoring, or aggressive the removal of a few outspoken individuals, only ninety-nine percent of the material they ruled unsuitable for public viewing could be guaranteed from reaching the public's domain. For the elite, the latent threat posed by the one percent that sneaked through was one that needed eliminating. 'The bastards policed it, filtered it and blocked it,' Art had informed Calvert a few years ago, 'and *still* their dirty little secrets kept springing up all over it.'

As it happened, the Dredge Wars were to take care of the problem for them, as on all reaches of the planet, global networks began to fail. Day by day the internet had become mysteriously infected with glitches, until finally it would cease to function at all. The prognosis from the world's experts was simply that it was a "casualty of war, and had died in action."

During the months following its demise, it was as though a light had been turned off. Businesses collapsed, birth rates increased—as did suicides. But in time, a government-controlled information platform would rise from the ashes like some third-rate phoenix. Christened *Insight Extra*, it was at best a diluted substitute, which could be likened more to a virtual library. Here, one could get news updates, limited pornography, check the weather and research certain subjects, but only the official (and usually fabricated) version. Gone was the ability to interact with others, let alone add anything yourself or challenge any of the findings already on there. There had been some backlash—a couple of half-hearted protests, but nothing of any real substance. Apathy would once again win the day, and eventually everyone just got on and accepted it.

Behind him, an outburst of heavy coughing rattled out, immediately snapping him from his thoughts. Upon turning around, he was just in time to witness the old man in the corner deposit a lump of phlegm into a cupped hand before wiping it down the front of his coat. It was at that moment Calvert decided he'd seen enough. Hastily finishing his drink, he slid himself from the barstool and headed straight for the door.

Outside, the bite of the cold air brought with it a small wave of relief as once more his feet hit the pavement. Any little enthusiasm he might have initially felt for his trip down memory lane was quickly ebbing away. There was nothing here for him anymore.

Deciding he would forgo the shuttle and walk the three miles home, he set off, pulling his jacket zipper up to its last notch. Passing two pleasure bars—The Orb and Jacob's Ladder—standing side by side on his left, he saw both establishments had queues beginning to form along the pavement. Business was obviously booming for some, or so it would appear. He also noticed that in the windows of both bars, in spindly pink neon lighting, the message 'Incorporating Vortex' informed potential clientele of something being offered inside which he himself was blissfully unaware of.

Breaking into a more positive stride, his hands sought refuge in the meagerly-lined pockets of his jacket. For now, his immediate need to keep them warm would have to override his craving for a cigarette. As he walked, his thoughts returned to The Marionette and the old man seated at the table. It was obvious now that it was *he* who was responsible for reigniting the dormant memory of a movie from over three decades prior. The resemblance to Jarvis—the captain of The Old River King—was minimal, but still enough to reopen a door in his mind which for many years had remained closed. What did this signify—if, in fact, anything at all? Something Calvert *was* certain of, however: he would never be crossing the threshold of his old haunt again. *That* particular door was one he would not be hurrying to reopen.

5

AutoButler v.3.1.7 - The AIR-Group Pat. No. 84828723 -
Assignment GH-22

Client log no. 9489b - Scan no. 6137

Body temp. check/normal - Pulse rate check/*abnormal, increased*
- Blood pressure check/*abnormal/increased* – high scan priority –
close observation mode engaged
   Suggested stimulus change: pattern-lighting-ambience/diffuse
relaxants deployed/initiate high scan/

It was time.

The naked figure in the chair finally completed what had been meticulous and time-consuming adjustments to the controls by his side, and now appeared ready to begin.

Emitting beams of light no thicker than a human hair, the AutoButler now began to methodically scan every inch of the man's flesh, before eventually adding the findings to its extensive memory banks. All vital signs were checked—the data analysed and automatically compared to information obtained just one hour earlier. Calculations to ascertain general condition, both mental and physical, would follow, all made in the blink of an eye.

SCRUTINISE—ANALYSE—OPTIMISE.

The rising blood pressure and quickening pulse were by now a familiar reading, but nonetheless still a cause for concern. Just to be thorough, the AutoButler ran a further digital probe procedure; as expected, the results confirmed the ones registered just five minutes earlier. Not only had the last few weeks proved to be a most valuable insight into its own abilities and limitations, but at the same time left it sufficiently rehearsed for the upcoming performance. For the present, there was little more it could do other than wait in Observation Mode—out of sight and mind—as it had done the previous time, and the time before that. As far as the AutoButler was concerned, this evening was to be business as usual, simply a repeat of the new normality.

As was by now becoming increasingly predictable, the man seemed composed at first, almost as though he was entering a deep state of sleep. However, within a couple of minutes, his behaviour began to show the first signs of regression, as a mild twitching at the corners of his mouth quickly escalated to a far more disturbing display. His long, stringy arms hanging limply down each side of the chair now jerked uncontrollably as muscle spasms began to rack his body. Before long, his breathing had become ragged and irregular—interspersed with guttural expletives as he writhed and twisted in the chair, as though caught in the grip of some hideous seizure. The problem for the AutoButler was that however efficient it might be, it was not programmed to intervene, and as such could do little more to assist without further instructions. For the time being, it would have to content itself with watching from above like some high-tech guardian angel, until it was time to check its master's vital signs once again.

The man's face, now swathed in a frenzy of flickering blue light, seemed somehow misshapen and grotesque. His thin lips were pulled back in what appeared to be an expression of pain, exposing his large and over-white teeth. Sweat glistened upon his brow as he threw his head backward over the top of the chair, emitting a loud groan. Nearly ten minutes had passed. It wouldn't be long now.

6

The man stirred and opened his eyes. Reaching up with an unsteady hand, he dragged the apparatus from his head, letting it fall to the floor beside him. Cautiously, he eased himself forward from the back of the chair until he was sitting in an upright position, where he stayed for a few minutes, rocking slowly back and forth. His eyes, now wide-open and jittery, skimmed the room as though the answer to his current predicament might be found in one of its shadowy corners. Even the subdued lighting could not dullen the sweat glistening on his shaved head, nor lessen the horrified expression that had taken possession of his face.

Gradually, fragments of lucidity began to return. With each passing second, the blurred edges were becoming sharper, his judgement clearer. This was his worst yet, no doubt about it.

Losing control was a concept relatively new to Gideon Hurst, and one which troubled him greatly. As a rationally behaved, logically thinking man, he'd never really understood the reasons why anyone would choose to distort reality—which, if he was to be honest with himself, was pretty much what he'd just been doing. Frantically, he now set about dissecting the contents of the Vortex's memory banks, scrutinising the data it provided—seeking the information that deep down he suspected he might already know. His fingers, usually so nimble and precise, now trembled as they erratically stabbed at and skidded across the touchscreen, the continual chore of having to re-enter the commands only serving to rankle him further. At last, the results materialised in front of him. The readings were not good. SPEED and INTENSITY set to maximum and the CONTENT SAFETY FILTERS all but disabled.

Now unable to sit still any longer, he prised his spent body from the chair and began to roam around the room, desperately trying to recall everything that had happened. There was little denying he'd been lucky this time. The data confirmed he'd blacked out after nine minutes and fifty-one seconds—very possibly saving his sanity in the process. Surely he wouldn't deliberately have set those parameters to such extremes, to then knowingly run the program with the content filters virtually deactivated? Hurst couldn't believe the risks he'd subjected himself to; his behaviour had been grossly irresponsible, verging on reckless—worse, maybe even the actions of a madman.

The ghastly sequence of images now began to replay in his mind, their sheer brutality surpassing anything he'd viewed so far. In hindsight, even he was forced to concede that the thoughts and memories of the late serial murderer Herbert Pamnent were not exactly what any well-balanced person could consider as healthy viewing. In fact, so abhorrent were the images, he wondered how anyone—himself included—could actually bear to peruse them. Was it at all possible that he himself could be equally as deviant and disturbed as Pamnent had been? Even safely within the confines of his own thoughts, the very suggestion was one which, up until now, he would have neither the self-awareness to recognise, nor the willingness to address. But surely they were hardly comparable? His own gratification—albeit far from normal—was purely from a voyeuristic perspective; his desire to watch another man's twisted and vile compulsions broke no law, and was therefore excusable. Although very aware his appetite for such depravity was on the increase, he'd also been reasonably successful in convincing himself it was most likely nothing more than a passing phase. Either that, or simply a normal reaction to the pressures of responsibility weighing too heavily on his shoulders. Now as he pondered the monstrous scenes of human carnage and suffering which had been dragged from inside Pamnent's head and into his own, Hurst was no longer able to deny that just maybe there were some issues which needed addressing. What he couldn't understand was how he'd allowed things to spiral so far out of control—to stoop to this level of degeneracy?

For a rash moment, he considered ridding himself of the machine altogether—of ordering Deeks to take it back to the AIR-Group headquarters for further investigation. As CEO of the Advanced Intelligence Research Group, Hurst was all too aware of the concerns expressed by a number of his colleagues regarding certain bonus features of the Vortex Subcon 2. He was, however, equally aware of its extreme selling potential, and as such, was reluctant to delay its release to an eagerly awaiting public.

In Hurst's judgement, this latest variant far exceeded the original model (now referred to simply as the MK-1) in every conceivable way. It was more compact—sleeker in design too, but by far its most enticing feature was its ability to manually override its own safety filters. Located in the machine's digital feed chain, once linked up to the recipient's subconscious, these had one function: to automatically register and then block anything considered too extreme, or even potentially dangerous, from getting through.

Although not a legislative requirement, the filters had been fitted to the MK-1 at the recommendation of the Vortex programme's chief technician Dr Van Dijk—a woman who, although undeniably gifted with a brilliant mind, in his opinion, sadly lacked ambition. Her overcautious (and somewhat myopic) conviction was that the consequences of permitting the unrestricted access of one man's thoughts to freely enter another's subconscious could have disastrous implications. To Hurst's dismay, Van Dijk's concerns were echoed by everyone on the board of directors but himself, whilst his own proposal—that of a function which enabled the user to run the program with the filters disengaged—firmly vetoed. It was the Councillor's unwavering belief that this had been a monumental error, and the only Achilles' heel of the MK-1. It was also one he was to make certain would not be repeated on the new and upgraded version. So this time around, assisted by much backstabbing in certain quarters, and a little palm-greasing in others, a four to one majority was to see him get his own way. Only Dr Yvette Van Dijk would not allow herself to be either bullied or bribed into submission, choosing to stand firmly by her principles. Whatever; it had made little difference to the outcome, which was clearly chalked up as a victory to Hurst. For the impending VS-2, the safety filters were to be redesigned and installed with a manual override option.

Although he would constantly insist that too much was censored in this delicate climate, and any restriction of the images were simply another infringement of customers' liberties, Hurst's motives were driven by the potential sales figures, and not principle as he liked to imply. That being said, the respect and admiration he would receive for being the mastermind behind the machine was what he hungered for, far above the obvious financial rewards generated by its success. This was the first time in his life he could remember feeling so close to possibly reaching this zenith, and for the past few months he had been the proverbial dog with a bone. No longer was the experience to be impeded by its previous limitations—legislation which, in his staunch belief, not only diluted the experience, but perhaps minimized its commercial appeal also. Despite the few teething problems which would continue to arise, he still had every faith that the VS-2 was only weeks away from its launch. The slogan to accompany this event—'Indulge in Unparalleled Sensory Overload'—had come to him in a fleeting moment of inspiration, inviting yet more reservations from his colleagues. But Hurst was nothing if not persistent, and as before, he'd eventually worn them down.

There was little doubt it would be declared the most advanced technology available in its field, and as such, its success was virtually guaranteed. No self-respecting pleasure bar would continue to run the older and inferior model once the VS-2 was unveiled—and he could personally testify to its addictive qualities. Who out there could possibly resist it? Surely the ultimate high had to be the ability to *unreservedly* look inside another man's psyche? To be able to access his thoughts, live his memories and share his deepest secrets, all with the comparable ease of turning the page of a book? The problem for Councillor Gideon Hurst was that whatever else was available to him, he always seemed to gravitate towards the *thoughts, memories and deepest secrets* of men such as Herbert Pamnent.

7

From across the open fields came the bitter northeasterly wind. Along the glassy, ice-covered pathways it swept, into the gardens and small backyards of Gunners Park—cold fingers which stirred and caressed. Nothing would remain untouched as it passed through.

Inside the workshop at the bottom of his narrow garden, Calvert had worked late into the night, heedless of its cries and moans outside his door. Above him, the tin roof rattled and the broken shutter banged repeatedly, but so engrossed was he in his work that he failed to notice.

Although small and rather primitive, the workshop was to become something of a sanctuary to him over the years—a place where victories, however insignificant, could be chalked up. Now at a little past 1am, the second wave of energy which had found him a couple of hours earlier was finally petering out.

The repairs to a neighbour's wind generator, now taking pride of place on his workbench, were all but done. To his surprise, installing the new bearings, although a lengthy task, had also proven to be a therapeutic one. Despite the advancing fatigue, he couldn't resist taking a minute or two to admire his efforts, spinning the now-smooth motor with no small sense of achievement. Debating whether to reassemble the blades before finally calling it a night, he'd decided against it, reasoning that it was a detail which could wait until daylight.

An hour later, and wide awake in his small back bedroom, he found himself unable to switch off the endless stream of thoughts spiralling round in his head. By now the wind had all but died away, leaving just the ticking of the clock beside his bed and the chattering from the poplar leaves outside his window to be heard. As he turned his pillow over yet again, he sighed in frustration at the prospect of another broken night's sleep. Where was the comfort the song of the trees usually brought to him—could it be that they too were losing their touch?

Calvert had always loved the wind, whether just a soft summer breeze upon his skin or a full-on epic winter onslaught. To him, it was one of the last touches of reality he could relate to in a world which, day by day, seemed hell-bent on becoming synthetically poisoned and technologically crippled. The very notion that it was a force too powerful to be changed or corrupted by the human race was one he was able to draw some reassurance from.

One night a couple of years ago, the winds were gale force across Gunners Park; such was their fury that they had actually howled. Lying there, tucked up, feeling the house tremble around him, he'd relished every sound and movement, despite his concerns over the damage he would inevitably find the following day.

But now, his mind was fixed on his son Elliot and the ever-expanding distance between them, the wide chasms he seemed unable to cross. Had he really done everything he could to resolve it?

Calvert was painfully aware that the fault lay primarily with himself and his inability to accept the rapidly changing times. Added to what he'd been told (on more than one occasion) was "an unrelenting determination to not fit in" and even he would struggle to deny that his company must, at times, be difficult for anyone close to him to tolerate. The problem was that, at forty-three years of age, he was still a relatively young man, yet old enough to have witnessed how things once were—comparisons he seemed unable to suppress in the rare conversations he would have with his son, often to the detriment of their limited time together.

Whether as a direct result of the 2026 Dredge Wars or not, Calvert firmly believed society had changed for the worse, rather than the better, as was widely believed by the majority of the population. However brightly coloured the government attempted to paint it (and admittedly some aspects would seem to have improved), it was a world he no longer recognised or felt any affinity towards. Yes, the streets might be safer; without doubt the hospitals ran with some level of efficiency at last, and homelessness appeared to have been virtually eradicated. Obviously there was no denying these things could only ever be regarded as steps in the right direction. So why then was he unable to see this evolution through more positive eyes? Deep within him, Calvert knew the answer—he had done for years. Basically, society functioned and that was all.

In spite of all the shortcomings associated with the twentieth century, there could be little dispute that the human race had taken a wrong turn since leaving it behind. Now over halfway through the next one, it was blatantly obvious to anyone paying attention that despite all the technological advances, modern civilisation was actually regressing. Maybe it did work more effectively now than it used to; very likely a certain section of the population were more affluent than they'd ever been. But something integral was missing. Where had the passion and spirit all too prevalent in his own youth gone? This was a question Calvert would keep returning to, automatically ruling out the possibility that his own viewpoint might have become coloured—or even completely distorted—with time. He'd long ago concluded it wasn't simply a case of a middle-aged man nostalgically looking back at his past through rose-tinted glasses, basking in the memories of his own halcyon days. No, it was more than that—much more. Why did no one feel the need to do things together like they used to? Even when in groups, nobody was ever really *together* in the proper sense. Yes, they might be sharing proximity to one another, but their interests would eventually come to be consumed by some handheld technology they seemed unable to exist without. It was almost as though wherever they happened to be, or whoever they happened to be there with, was not enough for them. Where was the human interaction that everyone at one time looked for, and seemingly found so impossible to live without? How can something like that just disappear?

As someone who had chosen to keep the world at arm's length, the hypocrisy of this particular sentiment was not lost on him. However, it was never Calvert's intention to distance himself from his fellow man—more the need to escape what he would come to regard as the trappings and absurdities of society. Never in any doubt his own needs for solitude were different from those of the majority, there was no escaping the fact that the end result was much the same.

While he would readily admit to being something of a loner, Calvert had never been aware of any actual feelings of loneliness—certainly not since those dark months immediately following the loss of his parents. There was always Art O'Sullivan for what he thought of as in-depth conversation, and small talk with strangers held little interest to him. While others felt the need to be surrounded by constant noise, his personal opinion was that great beauty often came wrapped in silence.

Yet, putting aside his own somewhat jaundiced perspective of mankind, he saw very little evidence of discontentment in others. They had their work, and plenty of money to spend in the pleasure bars or on the latest electronic devices, but was that necessarily an indication that everything was as good as it could be? How come no one ever asked *that* question? Did it mean everyone was actually fulfilled—or rather they'd stopped needing to be?

Maybe the problem really was with himself, as Kim would often make a point of alluding to, and not the world around him as he'd always led himself to believe. Whichever, there was one unanswered question that would continue to bother him; why had there been such rapid change over the last thirty years? Was it through natural progression, or by design? Just how responsible were the Dredge Wars for setting the pace and direction society was following? It was no good; his brain was now fully awake, his craving for a drink growing more impossible to ignore by the minute. Leaving the warmth of his bed, he groped around in the darkness for his socks, eventually finding them still inside the legs of his discarded trousers. Dragging the duvet from the mattress, he wrapped it around himself like a cloak, before padding down the short hallway to his kitchen and living area. After pouring himself a generous measure of scotch, he pulled a large photo album from his bookshelves and made himself comfortable on the chaise longue.

A few years back, suddenly recalling his late mother's inclination for detail and documentation, Calvert had removed all the photographs and turned them over, searching for clues. There, as suspected, was her distinctive slanted handwriting listing everything in blue ink—names, dates and places. Only the few from 2030 onwards remained blank.

Carefully, he now turned the heavy, dog-eared cover as he'd done so many times before, hoping to draw some reassurance from the familiar yet distant faces.

On the first page, pride of place went to Great Uncle William, even though Calvert had never even known him. A glossy, overly-coloured snapshot, only about three inches square, highlighted a young man barely out of his teens astride a large black motorcycle. His head was thrown back dramatically for the benefit of the camera, a cigarette dangling from the corner of his mouth, eyes squinting through the smoke that drifted upwards. Clean shaven with black hair greased and swept back from his face, the look was unashamedly Brando.

Calvert loved this photo, the unabashed cockiness verging on arrogance, belying the naïvety of a man as yet too young to have discovered how the world really worked. Indeed, William bore the expression so common to men of his age—one of an unswerving belief in themselves, something he himself would never get to experience during his own youth.

As a child, Calvert had lacked confidence in his own abilities, and never been the type to push himself in any of his studies. Always the underachiever at school, he would, years later upon his graduation into manhood, come to be regarded as something of an introvert by the few people who knew him. Was that necessarily a bad thing? He wasn't really sure, but had always believed that those who were would never be as likely to make their mark as the more outgoing type. Success favoured the extrovert, of that he was certain. Then again, so did everything . . . and everyone.

Studying a photo of himself aged eleven, he looked into the anxious face for any suggestion of the man he would later become, but it revealed nothing. Just a typical school photo, one which featured a rather insecure and unexceptional boy—someone who would pass quietly through life and no doubt leave in the same manner. Skipping forward a few pages, he found the only one of Kim, baby Elliot and himself all together. Elliot had only been a week or so old at the time, so pinpointing it to September 2036 was easy, even without confirmation on its reverse. Taken by Art in the small rear garden of number 7, on what was possibly the last Indian summer Calvert could remember, it was beautiful, both artistically and subjectively—the one photograph Calvert would inevitably find himself drawn to above all the others. Unfortunately, over the years, it was also to become something of a poignant memento. His younger self now seemed to stare back at him from behind the cellophane, the twenty-two year old eyes boring into his own. He wondered what the man in the photograph would say to him if he was able? *Look, this is what you once had, you stupid bastard—look.* He did look. For over five minutes he looked at nothing else. The three of them, huddled together on the rickety bench, Kim with her head on his shoulder, her face partly obscured by a mop of messy red curls. Between them, the newly-born baby was sleeping peacefully, wrapped against the first chills of autumn, a tiny blue bundle in her arms.

How could it all have gone so wrong? Could he have done anything to stop it falling apart? If so, why hadn't he even tried? These were the things he would ask himself often in the miserable days and months which followed. Again he studied the younger version of himself, searching for any indication of the cracks which would open up further down the line and throw his mind into such turmoil. Not only were there none to be seen, but the man in the photograph seemed to carry the air of one who believed he had struck gold. And that actually *was* how Calvert had felt at the time—happier than he could ever remember being. It really did all seem so perfect at first, as though all the missing pieces of his life were finally coming together. But sadly it wouldn't last. For Kim, the sedate lifestyle of Gunners Park was eventually to lose its lustre, until she found herself stifled by the quaint but makeshift little house, and the isolation that living there incurred. A lifestyle she'd once thought of as romantic in a chocolate box kind of way had, in reality, become little more than one of mundane predictability.

By that point, Calvert's growing aversion to socialising was impossible for her to ignore, only adding to the constant friction between them. Again and again she'd begged him to move the three of them to Mother City—to find a small apartment there, closer to her friends, "somewhere more fitting to raise a child." Eventually disappointment had turned to resentment, and still he wouldn't discuss it, choosing instead to simply extricate himself from the room whenever the subject would arise.

One evening on returning home, he'd found a note on the kitchen table. The short message, which even now he could recall word for word, was of little surprise to him. Strangely bereft of any real sense of loss, he'd carried on with his day-to-day routine, dead inside, with only that same hollow sense of indifference which had since grown to become a part of him. All the grief and remorse would remain, for the moment, still bottled up inside, quietly festering below the surface, biding its time. Kim and Elliot were gone, but it would be a little while before all those emotions would come to make their presence known.

The next photo was of a pale blue pickup truck belonging to Art O'Sullivan, parked up on a grassy bank, cleaned and posed for the event. He smiled at the sight of his own little four-year-old face peering through the cracked windscreen, remembering his childhood obsession with it. On the occasions when he'd been left in Art's care, the two of them would often drive the truck around Gunners Park—Art operating the pedals, with the tiny Calvert standing on the seat between his legs, hanging on to the steering wheel. Although his parents would have most probably been fine with it, the two of them had chosen to keep it as their secret. It was more fun that way.

The pickup was now over sixty years old, no longer blue, and pretty decrepit. However, O'Sullivan would never part with it, and up until recently could often be seen driving it around the estate. Like a few others who resided outside the city, he refined his own fuel from waste products in order to power it. As a practice, this was highly illegal, automatically incurring a hefty penalty if unfortunate enough to be apprehended by a Snooper. While some were deterred by this, others chose to throw caution to the wind and carry on regardless, adamant their lives would not be restricted by the fear of laws they believed to be unjust, or the marauding machines which upheld them. For Art himself, coming up with new ways to avoid them had been something of a sport—one he'd chosen to invest much time in. Thankfully they tended to keep to a set routine, which made this a relatively easy pursuit. With him being unlikely to venture into Mother City, and the Snoopers rarely patrolling as far out as Gunners Park, he would have been relatively safe as long as he didn't push his luck. Driving such a vehicle within the Inner or Outer Zones of the city was strictly prohibited, even when running on legally obtained fuel. Considered an act of sheer idiocy (even by Art), this particular legislation was rarely violated, as seizure of the offending vehicle would automatically result in its authorised destruction. However, it didn't end there. Within a few days, an unannounced visit from the military police would ensure the immediate ransacking of the miscreant's/victim's property, along with the probable confiscation of valuables to cover any costs which would have arisen while implementing the termination procedure. For Calvert, this was not something which was ever likely to affect him personally; he'd surrendered his license many years ago due to traffic violations. Since then, his point-blank refusal to pay the extortionate fees necessary to reclaim it had made certain that, for the foreseeable future, driving was not on his agenda.

Skimming through a couple more pages, Calvert paused at a photograph which never failed to intrigue him, one of only a handful there were of his father. Taken sometime in 2027; four men and a woman, all in early middle age, stood before a wall-plaque bearing the AIR-Group's red and black corporate logo, champagne glasses raised as they smiled towards the camera. Although he'd only ever known three of them, the other two were vaguely familiar to him, if by name only. From left to right he now studied them as he'd done on so many occasions. Arthur O'Sullivan, Dr Yvette Van Dijk, Francis Gorston, Councillor Gideon Hurst and Valentine Calvert.

Art didn't look that different, what must be close to being thirty-odd years ago. A few pounds heavier, for sure, and his hair was still dark, not yet ready to turn the silver grey it had been for as long as Calvert could remember. But still, he was instantly recognisable.

Hurst was another matter entirely. If not for the fact that he knew it to be him in the photo, Calvert would have never guessed the man's identity. Pencil-thin, with a side parting which did little to disguise the sparseness of his sand-coloured hair, there seemed to be almost a frailness to him. From his sloping shoulders, an ill-fitting suit hung in something of an apologetic manner, only serving to emphasise his leanness further. His lazy eye was scarcely evident though, leading Calvert to wonder why he'd bothered to adopt the eye patch in later years. Art's opinion was that it was just another of Hurst's many posturings, designed with the sole purpose of drawing attention to himself.

The photo had been taken to commemorate the launch of the company's first major government-sponsored project, their groundbreaking (if somewhat sinister) creation known simply as 'the Containment Wall'. Nowadays, these walls were commonplace on the landscape, dividing the countryside into many sectors. The technology involved in their conception may have been complex back in its day, but its function was straightforward enough—the prevention of contaminants, whether in the form of toxic air, viral contagion or disease being able to move from one area to another.

Calvert had a faint recollection of the wall materialising around Sector 21 (which the areas including and immediately surrounding Mother City were subsequently renamed), but at the time he'd not really been able to understand the probable ramifications. There was the odd demonstration from a minority faction, but the media was quick to ridicule the movement, instantly dubbing them the 'Anti Wallers.' These protestors had marched noisily past Calvert's house several times, chanting slogans—angry words which spoke of revolution and betrayal. Regardless, this would soon run out of steam when it became obvious that, to most people, the Containment Walls were of little concern. The fact that they no longer had the ability to leave their own sectors was a small price to pay for peace of mind and clean air.

Looking closely at his father standing far right, dressed in a crumpled white linen suit over a khaki t-shirt, Calvert realised how out of place he looked, the only one who appeared not to have made any effort in what was obviously a formal gathering. Leaning against the wall, nonchalantly gazing upwards, his demeanor was that of a man purely going through the motions. The other two, Gorston and Van Dijk, were of little interest to Calvert. He'd met them briefly many years ago; as far as he knew, they were still with the company.

He turned the thick leaves of the album until he came to the only photograph there was of his mother. Now studying it more thoroughly than he'd ever done before, he was struck by how little warmth or emotion it stirred within him. It wasn't just the way the shot had been taken either, it was . . . he tried to find the right sentiment . . . it was just *empty*. On reflection, it was probably quite an accurate representation.

His mother, although a very intelligent and admirable woman, had always been somewhat distant, as if displays of affection were unnatural to her. Yes, she'd loved him in her own way, but the relationship they shared was never a tactile one, unlike those he would witness between some of his friends and their mothers. At the time, he couldn't remember ever thinking he was missing out, but lately, for some reason he'd started to question why there had been so little tenderness.

He'd often thought it sad that Art had never been a father, although over the years Calvert would come to almost regard him as one. Art's take on the matter was he didn't think it was a world fit to bring children into, but Calvert suspected the real reason was he'd never been able to hang on to a relationship.

According to O'Sullivan, before the Dredge Wars it was not unusual for most couples to have children—sometimes even two or three, something which would be considered very strange today. But then again, so was much of what he talked about, especially when he'd been drinking.

Deciding it really wasn't worth going back to bed at this late hour, he poured himself another measure of scotch and lay back, his thoughts on Great Uncle William and what direction his life journey would most likely have ended up taking him. Just a teenage boy armed with nothing more than a tatty old motorcycle and an overconfident smile. A teenage boy whose only wish was to be Marlon Brando.

8

As per instructions, the young man rode the elevator to the first floor, thankful to find himself alone despite his anxiety at being in a confined steel box. His face, although pleasant enough, wore something of a haunted expression, its skin waxen and pallid, as colourless as the bones beneath it. Lank, dark hair poked from beneath a woolen skull cap, almost veiling the red-rimmed eyes which now skittered nervously across the bare grey walls, his fear of enclosed spaces glaringly obvious.

It's a metal coffin, maybe even hermetically sealed, certainly impossible to open from the inside in an emergency. The thought swam through his head before disappearing as the ride came abruptly to its end, the doors emitting a loud beeping as they opened. Although he was now at least a couple of hundred feet or more above ground level, the journey had probably lasted no more than about ten seconds in total—something of a relief to the young man.

Tentatively, he stepped out from the elevator and into the brightly-lit passageway beyond, patting down his pockets as a sudden surge of panic turned his stomach. His hands now began to scrabble frantically from jacket to trousers and back again, before eventually locating the folded application form. Breathing in deeply, he allowed himself a moment to refocus his mind—necessary seconds to adjust to his immediate surroundings.

Unusually, the walls to the corridor in which he now stood were curved, giving the impression of being inside a large tube, the surface of which appeared to be made of some kind of dull steel or possibly aluminium. Curiously, on touch, he discovered it to be warm and soft—more akin to the skin of a person. Ahead of him, directional signs hung in the air, green and ethereal as though formed from vapour. These he now followed, his eyes continuously switching from left to right, slightly intimidated by the array of severe-looking portraits which gazed back at him. The eyes of eminent scientists and revered philosophers all now seemed to follow him as he walked between them. Many he immediately recognised—such as Archimedes, Einstein and Copernicus; others were not quite so familiar, but all of them men, who through their own personal achievements had immortalised themselves. Little did they know all those years ago that the words which flowed from their pens would be quoted and speculated upon for eternity, their discoveries celebrated until the human race ceased to exist. But for now, they had all been brought together in this gallery of greatness, an overblown shrine of sepia and monochrome.

A couple of minutes later, just as he was approaching where he needed to be, he first experienced what he could only think of as a *connection.* It was the strangest feeling, not in any way unpleasant or threatening, but rather a sense of familiarity which he could not explain. There was nothing here he could possibly have seen before; it wasn't exactly a place you could visit one day and then forget you'd ever been. Whatever—with his mind the way it had been for the last few weeks, it wasn't something the young man would dwell on for long.

Rounding a corner, he discovered the corridor to be at its end, opening out into a circular waiting area with seating for approximately thirty people. About half the chairs were presently occupied. After a quick assessment of the room, he sat himself down, careful to avoid any eye contact as he did so, deliberately positioning himself as far from anyone as was physically possible. Unfolding the application form, he skimmed his eyes across the print, only to find that his present level of anxiety would prevent him from actually absorbing any of the information. However, grateful for anything which might serve as a distraction, he buried his face in its crumpled facts and figures.

The silence was eventually broken by the bestial grunts of a small and rather unruly child opposite him, and the mother's attempts at calming it. Shushing impatiently through swollen, collagen-filled lips, her efforts—if anything—appeared to be having the opposite effect. Writhing and twisting furiously beneath her grasp, the tiny red-faced creature would not be silenced by either her hissing displeasure or furious glare. The young man watched the display with growing alarm, instantly repelled by the woman, yet at the same time unable to look away. There was definitely something about her pouting, over-painted face which even in his present fragile state he found fascinating.

Shaved to within a gnat's cock of total baldness, her head appeared to be uneven, almost to the point of being lumpy. At first he wondered whether she was inflicted with some horrific medical condition, before realising it was nothing more than the result of subdermal implants. Despite the warmth of the room, he felt a shiver pass through him.

Don't look into her eyes; you might see things best left unseen.

Thankfully, the child's attempts to break free seemed, at least for the moment, to have been effectively thwarted. It now lay across her lap, whining, its angry little hands eagerly snatching at the chocolate bar which now hovered six inches from its snotty nose, as if with the sole purpose to torment. Seated on her left, and apparently oblivious to the events, was what he could only presume to be the father. Overweight and sweating profusely, he was slumped back against the wall, his flabby wet mouth open, gaping like some hideous bloated fish. Perched above his pudgy nose, the lenses flickered randomly, showering him in a vibrant blue. His appearance only served to agitate the young man further.

Swim, blue fish. Swim away, blue fish. You are the sweatiest blue fish in this big, grey tank.

From time to time, his shiny, pig-like head would roll from one shoulder to the other, incoherent mutterings his only contribution to the proceedings. Wherever his mind was, it certainly wasn't here.

The young man found himself wondering what these two people could possibly see in each other. Surely to be alone would be a preferable option to what he concluded could only be a miserable union? Whatever; at least now the child was still. Pacified by the chocolate its mother had eventually relinquished, it now permitted silence to return to the room.

Run, little child, run. Get out while you can. Believe me, it only gets worse.

On the other side of the mother, wearing a faded military-style tunic, an elderly gentleman sat perched on the edge of his seat, eyes closed as his liver-spotted head nodded dreamily to whatever thoughts were passing through it. Reaching up with a bony hand, he began to caress the remnants of his thin, white hair, a dreamy smile settling upon his mottled face. The young man wondered absently if he was someone's grandfather, deciding maybe that was something else missing from his own life.

Glancing back at the young family, he was relieved to see the child appeared to be on the verge of falling asleep. While the mother sat upright, inspecting her fingernails, the father had sunk into his seat, face lowered to his chest. The blue lenses still glowed, although they seemed to have slipped down his nose and now rested at an angle.

That's enough, stop looking at them. It's only making you worse.

He jumped as a loudspeaker fixed to the ceiling emitted a short ping, followed by a synthesized female voice. 'Howard Crane to the recreation suite please, Howard Crane.' It wasn't for him.

At the mention of his name, the old man glanced around him as if to seek reassurance he'd heard correctly. When none was offered, he rose cautiously to his feet, his deep-set eyes fixed on the wall opposite the room's entrance where a previously concealed doorway had just revealed itself. Each step was measured as he now shuffled towards it, his head still nodding as he disappeared from view. As though mesmerised by the pendulous, reedy figure, the young man found himself unable to look away. Not until the closing doors became a gap, a line, then nothing, would he turn his attention back to the questionnaire, before a rerun of bellyaching from the child—awake once more, courtesy of the loudspeaker—rendered this futile. Thankfully, a second bar of chocolate rapidly materialised and all was quiet again. Relieved, he leaned back in his seat, telling himself he would most likely be next in line . . .

Just as his mind was beginning to slip into that strange place between sleep and wakefulness, his name was finally called out. Not the one given to him at birth, but rather another he had opted to sign in with—a moniker designated solely for the few occasions like this, when he felt anonymity to be a wise precaution. Startled, he jumped up, stuffing the application form into his pocket as he stumbled towards the waiting doorway. It took him just a few seconds to cross the floor, but still long enough for his mind to visualise the horror of it closing before he could reach it, and therefore depriving him of the opportunity which lay beyond.

Safely through it, he immediately found himself confronted with an immense wall, its size and curvature such that it gave the impression of something which had naturally swollen rather than having been intentionally built that way. Like the outside of the tower, it too seemed to be made of some kind of aluminium. At regular intervals, reinforced perforated columns protruded from its surface, a number of which were positioned more closely together than the others, breaking the otherwise uniformity. Between these, eight cylindrical compartments, about six feet in height, were recessed. The door to each one was presently open, the inner walls heavily padded, and very obviously a form of elevator. Unlike any lift he'd used previously, their entrances were narrow, barely wide enough for a person to squeeze through into the cramped space beyond. Looking up into the void above him, he could determine that he was now inside some kind of vertical shaft, the top of which at present was impossible to see.

From somewhere within the surrounding expanse, a male voice now broke through the distant echoes of machinery at work. Not the dull, artificial announcement he was expecting, but one which actually projected a modicum of warmth and humanity.

'Welcome to the AIR-Group. We are dedicated to making your experience a pleasurable and rewarding one. Please step into one of the transportation modules and use the handrails provided at all times. You are about to enter Level One.'

Clambering into the nearest capsule, he wrapped his fingers around the cool steel bars, his touch upon them instantly followed by the clicking of micro-switches engaging somewhere beneath his feet. With barely any room to move, the close proximity of the cushioned interior was suffocating, despite the series of ventilation grills which encircled his head.

'Finally, please enter the six digit code from your application form into the control panel in front of you.' The voice was pleasant, not an order so much as a cordial request. Where might he have heard it before?

The young man had his numbers saved to memory, and now carefully tapped them in, just as was requested of him. He then waited, wondering what further instructions would follow. But there were none, only the dull click of his door locking itself in preparation. At the sound of electric motors suddenly kicking in, he now found himself gripped by conflicting senses of both elation and fear. Yes, he might have achieved something of a personal milestone by even getting this far, but it was also the point of no return.

Relax, man, none of this is real, and even if it is, what have you got left to lose, hey?

The module shuddered, the movement barely detectable, but enough to alert him that he was now in motion. The inertia he'd imagined would send his stomach to his boots was, in reality, pretty much non-existent, something which in different circumstances might have come as something of a disappointment. A minute later and his instincts were telling him he was no longer climbing vertically, but had branched off at an angle. Peering out through the tiny perspex windows, he looked for confirmation of this, but there was nothing much to see, only the blur of the surrounding walls as they sped by. Lifting his eyes to the vast emptiness above, he could see a soft violet glow beginning to creep in via a formation of opaque glass portholes, a light which turned his skin a purplish blue as he ascended into it. Holding his hands up in front of him, he smiled as he studied them, becoming quite absorbed in the unexpected change of colour. It was as he looked back up that it suddenly hit him—the higher he was climbing within the shaft, the narrower it was becoming also, gradually closing in until there was virtually no space between its walls and his module.

Now on the verge of a panic attack, the young man began to break out in a cold sweat, his heart rate increasing rapidly as he fought to calm himself. From somewhere, he heard a voice scream out for the ride to end, and realised it was his own. Unable to prevent the rampaging of his mind, he instead did what he always did in times of distress—he screwed his eyes firmly closed and counted.

One . . . two . . . three . . . four . . . five . . . six—

He got no further before the hum from the motors began to lighten, indicating that the module was decelerating. It now coasted silently for the short remainder of the journey until finally coming to rest at its destination. At the sudden loss of momentum, he reopened his eyes to discover he was in the centre of a large, disc-shaped room. It was at that point he knew he'd just arrived at Level One.

71

Behind the perspex windows, he found that by twisting his head around, he was presented with a three hundred and sixty degree perspective, which he now scanned nervously. With not one wall or even a partition to obstruct his line of vision, or diminish the room's 'hollowness', the circular expanse which now surrounded him seemed colossal. In every direction, figures moved back and forth, engaged in various undefinable activities, each dressed in either green, red or blue scrubs, quite possibly denoting department or status.

Releasing his grip of the handrail, he uncurled his stiff white fingers, wiping their dampness down the front of his jacket. Without another thought, he placed his palm firmly upon the door and stepped out.

Hearing it close behind him, the young man turned and watched his module leave, no doubt heading back into the darkness below, where it would wait with the others before returning with the next deadbeat. He shuddered, wishing he was somewhere else—anywhere else; the pleasure bars, his tiny miserable apartment, even. At that moment, just treading the cold city streets suddenly seemed more attractive than ever before. However irrelevant his life might be, he was suddenly desperate to return to it, to cocoon himself in its safe and familiar tedium. But, in doing so, he would be forfeiting his means to a recently discovered infatuation, and the much needed fogginess it brought to him. The daily grind of the nine to five would have to be endured without it coursing through his bloodstream to mask the misery and hopelessness of everything. Could he really do that? More to the point, was there good enough reason to? Just lately he'd been reflecting on his recent change of circumstances—the direction he'd so willingly taken—and was very aware his present predicament could not be a sustainable one. However, there were no other options he could think of worth pursuing, at least none which could offer anything that even remotely interested him. For better or for worse, this was it—all that remained open to him, and if nothing else, would hopefully buy him a little more time to find an alternative. Just once couldn't hurt, surely?

9

By the time Calvert stepped through the door, Kim was already there. Perched on a tall chair by the furthest window, in what they used to refer to as 'their spot' all those years ago, she looked different to when he'd last seen her—almost sophisticated with her auburn hair piled high upon her head. As yet she appeared not to have noticed his arrival, smiling as she shared a thought with someone or other via the tiny electronic gadget she now held pressed to her forehead.

Cautiously, he weaved his way towards her around the small solitary tables, each one partially surrounded by a shield of black perspex, designed in such a manner as to provide the occupant with at least a modicum of privacy. Behind one of the darkened screens, a silhouette droned technospeak into one of the provided headsets, while another dispensed a melange of digital beeping and white noise. Not for the first time, he wondered why anyone would come to a public place, only to seek solitude once there. Approaching the mini bar area where Kim was seated, he could see the all too commonplace blue light flickering sporadically between her fingers, speeding up as she laughed. Long-dormant feelings of jealousy now began to awaken within him as he wondered who she could be sharing her thoughts with—who it might be that was able to amuse her like he'd once been able to.

Sitting himself down beside her, he noticed her face seemed a little flushed as she hurriedly attached the gadget to a strap wrapped around her wrist.

'Hi, Marcus.' The smile was sincere enough, but nothing more.

He returned the greeting, surprised at how awkward he felt in her company after all this time. How long had it been since they last met? Must be a couple of years, surely—possibly even closer to three, so why the sudden urgency to speak to him now?

Although fully aware of the formality a separation inevitably brings, Calvert would never really come to terms with the space which now existed between them. 'Strangers with a past' was how he'd once rather flippantly summed up the relationship to Art during one of their whisky-fuelled conversations. To himself, he was forced to admit it was emotionally more complicated than that—for him, anyway.

Having just started her drink, Kim declined his offer of another, and he turned his attention to the mini screen in front of them to place his order. Calvert hated these things and, unless desperately needing the particular service they happened to provide, would opt to go without rather than subject himself to the horror of having to use them. His fingers now poked clumsily at the beeping screen, unable to silence it, the irritating flashing box containing the word *ERROR* refusing to yield to his efforts. He started again, now stabbing irritably at the tiny buttons, missing the ones he intended to hit, by now completely humiliated by his own fumbling ineptitude.

Kim watched his failed attempts for a while, a look of bemusement forming on her face. Despite having witnessed similar performances from him many times in the past, she still couldn't help but be astonished at his inability to carry out even the most basic function where anything screen-related was concerned. This was so typical of him, a frustration that quickly turned to anger at anything he didn't understand.

She'd long ago come to realise she would probably never understand the inner workings of Marcus Calvert—however, there was one little quirk in particular which had always struck her as even more peculiar than the others. How was it that when it came to technology, he could fix it but not operate it? It simply defied all logic. There was no doubting that in this particular field of expertise, he was possibly unique, and most definitely a living contradiction.

It was largely this pig-headed determination to stay firmly rooted in the past, dogmatically rejecting anything which could be considered even slightly progressive, which would eventually drive a wedge between them. To a woman who was quite content to just accept whatever direction the world happened to be steered in, and not look too deeply into how and why, his innate mistrust of everything around him had been tiring to live with.

Leaning across, she tapped a code into the electronic menu and hit the assigned ORDER button. 'Same old Marcus,' she teased. 'I assumed it would still be white, two sugars?'

Calvert winced. Was he really that predictable?

Nodding in reply, he asked himself if predictability was such a bad attribute? Maybe, but he could certainly think of worse traits.

Seconds later, a trolley bearing his order scooted across the floor and pulled up next to them, an annoying, high-pitched whistling alerting him to its arrival. 'Your order, sir. Please enjoy,' it squawked in a thin, artificial voice.

For once, Calvert kept his opinions regarding the Novum Bar's policy of using automatons rather than employing humans to himself, opting instead to simply glare at it with suspicion. Hopefully it would pick up on his negativity before attempting to break into some inane, generic conversation. Reaching down to retrieve his coffee from the dreadful thing, he remained silent while in its presence, heedful of Art's warning that all machines, whatever their official stated purpose, listened in to your conversation. For no apparent reason, it continued to just sit there, until it suddenly dawned on him that it was expecting a tip. It wasn't going to happen.

Calvert rapped his knuckles upon its shiny stainless steel surface. 'We're done here, you can sod off now,' he informed the trolley. 'Go on, take a hike.'

At his obvious displeasure, it scuttled away again, emitting another ridiculous whistle before disappearing into a hole in the wall, taking with it his desire to smash it to pieces with a large hammer.

'It's Elliot,' Kim blurted out suddenly.

'What is?' Calvert shook his head, attempting to clear his mind of the odious trolley.

'He's on something, I know he is. He's so . . .' Kim dropped her gaze to her hands, now locked together on the narrow ledge in front of her. 'He's stick-thin and . . . his eyes, well, you know . . . they look terrible. He's hardly eating or keeping himself clean. I'm really scared for him.'

Calvert absorbed her words, played them over in his head, already beginning to feel very much out of his depth. He nodded slowly, his attention becoming drawn to the glass which sat in front of her, its contents the same murky grey and insipid liquid those kids in The Marionette had been drinking. *What was it?* he wondered absently. It looked foul. 'Drugs, you mean? No, I can't see it myself. It could be anything.' He frowned and looked back at her. 'Are you sure?' Even while the question was leaving his mouth he realised how feeble it sounded, how unlikely she was to be mistaken.

'Of course I'm bloody sure, Marcus. I see enough of him to notice something like this.'

Calvert held his hands up in front of him in a gesture of appeasement. 'Okay, okay, I'll talk to him, I promise. Try not to stress too much, Kim, you know what kids can be like—all these weird phases they go through.'

She softened a little. 'He's hardly a kid anymore. He'll be twenty-two this year.'

Ever conscious that last year he'd completely forgotten Elliot's twenty-first birthday, Calvert once again felt the return of prickling pangs of guilt. Hopefully, Kim wouldn't decide this to be the appropriate time to also bring up the six months or more which had slipped by with no attempt on his own part to make contact with him.

In all fairness to himself, during the first couple of years after Kim and Elliot had left, he'd been every bit the dutiful father. Admittedly, his radical improvement was largely brought about by his hoping that such displays of atonement might eventually bring them both back to him. However, it wasn't to be, and as Elliot entered his teenage years, for him, the novelty of alternate weekends spent in Gunners Park would begin to lose their appeal. Days spent building dens, exploring the old industrial estate, and nights camping in the woods were becoming something of a chore for the boy, a ritual of duty which was to gradually decline as the months turned to years. Elliot had changed, moved on forward, eager and receptive to the modern technological age which Mother City offered, while leaving his father firmly rooted in the past, the product of a bygone age.

Now at forty-three and twenty-one years of age, it was as though they no longer had anything in common with each other. On the rare occasions they did meet up, their conversation was stilted, consisting mostly of small talk. With neither of them able to find common ground where they could connect, these get-togethers would usually end prematurely, having lapsed into an uncomfortable silence. Typically, several hours afterwards, Calvert would be full of self-reproach for his failures, vowing to himself that next time around he would do better. But he never did; instead, he'd opted to do very little, convinced in his naïvety that the problem would naturally remedy itself. Time was to prove otherwise; if anything, the situation had only deteriorated further. If he was to be brutally honest with himself, it wasn't something he'd given a great deal of thought to for quite a while.

Now, as Kim poured her heart out, he listened attentively, quite prepared for the finger of blame which at any moment could come to rest in his direction. For the next half an hour she reeled off the changes in their son, never once reminding him of his parental shortcomings, or the disappointment which he knew she harboured.

Only when she was finished did Calvert express his alarm, no longer in any doubt that Elliot had fallen prey to the opioid epidemic which first crept into the city a couple of years earlier.

'So, what do we do?' Kim was pushing now, her eyes boring into his, demanding more than he was presently giving. 'Whatever it takes, this really does need sorting now.'

Calvert nodded and said all the right things which sprung to mind, promising he would act right away, reassuring her all would be okay. Aware that his words seemed to be bringing her some comfort, his confidence in his own ability to resolve the situation was escalating by the minute. It had been so long since she'd valued either his opinion or input in anything, he'd almost forgotten how good it could make him feel.

Eventually, she seemed to have emptied herself of everything she needed to say, and Calvert began to sense the rendezvous drawing to its conclusion. 'Thank you, Marcus,' she responded, the gratitude evident in her voice. 'It really has been good to see you again, I mean it.' This time the smile was warmer and he returned it—a fleeting moment, but long enough for it to stir something within him. Feeling a little foolish, he began to fumble in his jacket pocket on the pretext of searching for something. When he looked up again, it was to see her face clouding over as her tone once more became serious. 'Just don't forget, okay? I'm depending on you, so please, whatever you intend to do, it needs doing straight away.' She climbed down from her chair and retrieved her coat from beneath the countertop, happy to let him help her into it—something he would automatically have done when they first got together, a time before all the rot set in. To him now, those days seemed so distant, almost as if they had never really existed; like memories which belonged to somebody else, that somehow he'd been privy to. She reached up to give him a token peck on the cheek, smiled once more, and was gone.

He watched her through the window, his eyes following her petite figure until it was swallowed up by the crowd, disappearing—along with his hope that she might glance back over her shoulder.

10

The room was nothing like he'd imagined. Not that the young man held any preconceived idea of quite what to expect; there were certainly no past experiences from which he was able to draw any comparison. Despite the enormity of the floor area, its ceilings were low and slightly oppressive, their surface a mass of tiny, honeycomb-shaped holes allowing a soft-yellow light to filter downwards. The floor beneath him appeared to be made of some kind of a steel mesh, through which a multitude of horizontal chromium rods were just visible. Along these, balls of blue light were travelling silently back and forth in a uniformly manner, lighting up the darkness underneath as they moved. The perimeter of the room was surrounded by dozens of translucent windows, concave and ovaloid in shape, about four feet in diameter. He was instantly reminded of the inside of eggshells which had been sliced in half, and realised these were what, as a child, he would often think of as resembling insect eyes when viewing them from the street below.

'Life pods for children,' his father had once told him as they passed by on their way back from school. 'It's where they sleep and grow.'

Looking back, he was never quite sure which one of them was responsible for actually naming it the Pod Tower, only that for him the name would stick, not just back then, but ever since. Frequently it was to be the theme of his childhood stories; many of them he could still recount—and with surprising clarity, almost as though they had been told to him that very same day. One in particular would still visit him in his dreams from time to time, the effects of which could leave him disoriented for hours upon awakening, without actually having any idea why. Although this particular segment of his past seemed a lifetime ago, it was still easy to recall when it was most likely to have first started—the spark which lit the fuse, so to speak.

It was the year before he and his mother had finally left Gunners Park, their big move to the city, so he couldn't have been more than six years old. Along with two or three other kids from the estate, he would board the school shuttle each morning, and at the end of the day be returned the same way. But every now and then, as he exited the school gates, it was to find his father waiting to collect him, and instead, he would climb up onto his shoulders for the journey home. From here he could see everything there was to see. Nobody on Earth was as tall. He was a giant roaming his kingdom, omnipotent and immortal, righting the wrongs which others brought to the world. But best of all was the moment when they would pass beneath the dark, brooding tower, where inevitably his eyes would climb the grey metal monster all the way to its pinnacle, before letting go. Little did he know that long after it had ceased to take precedence in both sight and mind, it would still remain within him, putting down a few more roots in his already fertile imagination.

On reflection, it was obvious it had been something of an obsession to him, undoubtedly fuelled even further by the stories told to him on those rare but memorable occasions. The seed that was the Pod Tower had been given life, and would continue to grow until eventually filling the boy's young, impressionable mind with both fear and fantasy alike. A surrogate reality was to eclipse all others, one in which the two levels with their rows of pod-like apertures would come to be the focal point for his thoughts. In particular, it would be the upper level which held the most fascination for him, as it was where the old wizard lived.

At night, this mysterious, bearded figure would roam the tower on a flying chair, while in the life pods, his children would sleep peacefully until the sun reached inside to wake them. The lower level was reserved for the servants and their children who cooked and cleaned for him, attending to his every need. In later years, the young man had become conscious of an underlying malevolence—albeit an unintentional one—which often accompanied these stories. It was odd, but standing here now, despite being able to see that his pods were nothing more than windows, looking at them still gave him a sense of unease.

His thoughts were interrupted by a middle-aged, rather sour-faced woman dressed in green hospital scrubs who suddenly appeared by his side, a clipboard pressed to her chest, above which a badge informed him she was an 'Imaging Technician'.

'Mr. Morrison?' she enquircd, peering at him from over the top of her spectacles before consulting her paperwork. 'Two-thirty procedure?'

He nodded, relieved the pseudonym he'd used earlier had once more bypassed any suspicion.

'Okay, sir, please follow me.' She spun around sharply and headed away without once looking back, her speed and agility at odds with her large frame. Falling in behind her, he allowed himself a brief sideways glance at the rows of identically-clad figures, hunched over computer workstations. Tapping away furiously, as though their very lives depended on it, not one of them so much as lifted an eye in his direction.

Reaching the outer perimeter of the room, the assistant stopped at a row of peculiar-looking chairs which were positioned facing inwards. Those presently in use were reclined, their raised sides reminiscent of chrysalides, or shiny black pea shells which had been split open. His view of anyone currently occupying them was partially obscured by wires and other apparatus, but all seemed to be asleep and under no duress at all. Silent and still, they were almost corpse-like; arms crossed neatly across their chests. Next to each chair, an extensive bank of switches and dials was mounted beneath an array of miniature, hemispherical monitor screens. Some featured blurry images shifting around on them, but all of them too amorphous for him to possibly decipher.

'Please make yourself comfortable, Mr. Morrison.' The orderly pointed towards a vacant chair. 'I will be with you shortly.'

Stepping up onto the raised footboard which ran all the way around it, the young man reached out for the small grab rail, cautiously lowering himself in. Within seconds he began to feel suffocated, his movements quickly becoming restricted as malleable leather automatically adjusted itself to the contours of his body.

They're wrapping you up, mate. Soon you won't be able to breathe. I told you this was a bad idea, didn't I?

Leaning his head back upon the generously padded support, he took a series of deep breaths, telling himself he could do this, willing himself to become calm. Before long, the chair began to lose some of its constrictive feel, and he found himself enough at ease to take an interest in what was going on around him. On the opposite side of the room, from what appeared to be some kind of elevated stage, a tall man with a shaved head and eye patch observed the proceedings with a rather superior expression. Occasionally, he would call out an instruction to one of the many orderlies and technicians working below, a gloved finger pointing in their direction as he spoke. Around him, a plethora of computer screens flickered madly, while behind, a backdrop of digital projections mutated. Showered in vibrant-coloured light, there was an almost rockstar-like persona about him as he strutted back and forth, his large hands clasped behind his back.

It's him, look! It's that guy Hurst who your dad knows. Game's up now, mate.

Although aware the Councillor was connected to the AIR-Group, the thought that he might be here today and very obviously in charge, wasn't one the young man had even considered. Now as Hurst's gaze came to rest in his direction, he felt his heartbeat begin to quicken, before reassuring himself that his fears were irrational. There could be no way the thin man on the stage could possibly recognise him after all this time.

Although several years since last setting eyes on the Councillor, he had a vague recollection from his early childhood days of him being a friend of his father, but not so much his mother. It was surprising how little he'd changed; a little gaunt perhaps, but as upright and fit-looking as ever despite his advancing years. The air of authority was still just as prominent, the demeanor of someone comfortable not only in his surroundings, but also his own skin. Eventually, and much to the young man's relief, the Councillor spun himself around before striding across his platform to lean over the balcony and fix his stare elsewhere.

Just as he was beginning to think he'd been forgotten, his technician returned, wheeling a surgical trolley on which some unfamiliar medical items were laid out neatly upon a white sheet. Accompanying her was an older woman who introduced herself as Dr Van Dijk. Pleasant-looking, with long, greying hair tied up into a bun, the warmth she projected seemed almost out of place here.

He nodded his head in acknowledgement, briefly scanning the instruments, but registering only the syringe which now seemed to stare back at him with all the menace of a loaded gun.

The technician smiled thinly. 'Try and relax, Mr. Morrison, it will all be over soon.'

Shifting himself in the chair, he looked away from her, opting to stare straight ahead at an assortment of controls and tiny flashing lights. Under the watchful eye of her superior, she now retrieved a dozen or so coin-sized rubber pads from the trolley, and after parting his matted hair, one by one proceeded to place these onto various parts of his head. Not until they were all in their desired positions did she then press down firmly onto each one, the tiny pins located on their surfaces drawing blood as they punctured his skin. Attaching a cluster of wires to them, she then stretched a latex skull cap over everything, adjusting it until finally she was satisfied that all was as it should be. 'Are you fully aware of the procedure we will be carrying out today, Mr. Morrison?'

But the young man was still focused on her previous comment. *It will all be over soon—that's what she said just now, wasn't it?* Shutting the thought from his mind, he nodded his head feebly as confirmation.

Handing him the consent form to sign, she then went on to explain about how it was a 'relatively straightforward and painless procedure, nothing for him to feel the slightest concern over,' before adding that 'obviously the AIR-Group could not be held accountable for any adverse side effects incurred afterwards.'

Signing it without so much as glancing at anything written there, he hastily passed it back to her.

'In just a minute, Dr Van Dijk will administer a small injection,' she continued, busying herself with the items on the trolley. 'I can assure you, it's really nothing to worry about, just a little something to help coax those memories from the subconscious to the conscious.' She tested the syringe, flicking it before dabbing something cold on his arm. 'Do you have any questions before we begin?'

Now's your chance! Go on, ask her! Did she really just say it will all be over soon? What the hell does that mean? Surely you're not going to just let that one pass?

As the doctor took the syringe from her colleague and moved forward to take over, the young man said nothing. Instead, he just shook his head and mentally prepared himself for the needle which was now hovering just above his vein.

'Okay, Mr. Morrison, it will not hurt, you have my assurance. I've done this many times, believe me.' Van Dijk's voice was reassuring and almost motherly, with the hint of an accent he couldn't place. Screwing his eyes firmly closed, he pushed his head back into the soft leather of the chair, his clenched jaw pressing his teeth tightly together. This was a mistake, he shouldn't be here—maybe he could simply apologise for wasting their time and leave? Beside him he could just make out the hushed voices of instructions being passed back and forth, the details impossible for him to comprehend. A brief silence followed before he felt the gentle touch of a latex-covered hand against his skin.

Jesus, I can't believe you're gonna let her stick that fucker in your arm. You must be mad. You don't even know what's in it!

To his surprise, it wasn't anywhere near as bad as his memory had let him believe it would be. In fact, it was practically painless—obviously another one of those groundless fears which had, over time, grown out of all proportion. Gradually his mind and body seemed to switch off, as though being emptied of all rational thought. Beneath him, he felt the chair recline further, its sides closing in a little more to encase his body like a soft, leather coffin. Then he heard the voice, dreamy and seductive in his head. *'Think about your first sexual experience and share it with me please.'* Just as he was wondering whether he'd imagined it, there it was again. *'Please, your first sexual experience, think about it and share it with me. I need to know all about it.'*

This would be easy. It could only have been a couple of years before, and was therefore still fresh in his mind. Since then, aside from the occasional dalliances with cheap-rate prostitutes on his housing estate, there had been no others.

Her name was Abi Soames—and to use an expression of his mother's, she'd already "got something of a reputation". For days after the deed, his friends were to amuse themselves with the rumour she was still only fifteen years of age, something which had somewhat marred his memory of the occasion. Thankfully for him, this would come to be dismissed as untrue by her best friend, but not until nearly a week of torturing himself had passed. He'd genuinely really liked her, but was too self-conscious to pursue a relationship, opting instead to give into peer pressure from the group of young men he'd hung around with. In hindsight, he could see what an immature and pathetic bunch of cocks they really were, but at the time it was easier simply to push her away rather than face their ridicule.

Now, once more, he was experiencing it all over again—only in his head, maybe, but every bit as real as when it had actually happened. Her smooth skin responding to his touch, her firm body writhing beneath him, was his last conscious *and* subconscious thought. A thought he would never again have the pleasure to recall—one he would be unaware had even existed to begin with.

Elliot Calvert had not only just relived one of his most precious memories, he'd also unknowingly sold it for the price of two weeks' rent.

11

When Art O'Sullivan eventually answered his door, it was obvious to Calvert that he'd just woken him. His eyes, narrow and dulled from sleep, peered out into the darkness, his only expression one of momentary confusion. Even beneath the feeble glow of the porch light, his deterioration since they'd last met was painfully evident. Leaning on the doorframe for support, his once-wide shoulders now drooped beneath the striped blanket wrapped around them. It was the carriage of a man with little fight left in him, a body which now seemed to have resigned itself to the unthinkable. This was the moment Calvert first became aware that not only had Art's physical appearance changed, but so too had his demeanour. It was almost as though he was looking at someone else, somebody he no longer recognised.

Beckoned inside without so much as a word, Art led him down the dimly-lit hallway and into the large, farmhouse-style kitchen where he tended to spend most of his time. Following behind, Calvert couldn't fail to notice how slow his movements were—how heavy his breathing was. But above everything, the one thing he could not believe was how much this once-large man had diminished in size. Shuffling over to the sink, Art reached for a copper kettle and proceeded to fill it, leaving him to make his way over to the table and take a seat.

While O'Sullivan busied himself with the teapot, Calvert looked around him. Something was different, although he couldn't work out what it was. As always, he ran an admiring eye across the grey-slate flooring, towards the wall just above the countertop where three stained glass windows dominated the white shiplap. Arched and traditionally edged with lead, they had what he'd once thought as something of a 'churchy' appearance—a viewpoint which was to rapidly change the first time he'd taken notice of the scenes depicted within them, and realised just how unholy they actually were. Now, with only the darkness behind them, they were virtually colourless, as though they too had given up on life. How different they'd looked last summer with the evening sun pouring through them, washing the kitchen in brilliant blue, red and green light. But it wasn't just the windows, nearly everything in here would have been made by Art—the units, the shelves, even the massive kitchen table. Now looking at him shambling across the floor, a mug of tea in each hand, it was difficult to imagine.

As hard as it was to watch, Calvert knew better than to offer his assistance, having recently made that mistake and been sworn at as a reward. As the old man eased himself into a chair, he winced as if in pain, pulling his blanket tightly around him, seemingly oblivious to the warmth from the enormous, wood burning stove.

'Marcus.' He looked up in acknowledgment, the tired smile failing to lift the deep creases beneath his eyes.

'How are you, Art?' There was no getting around asking this, but even as the words left his mouth, Calvert hated himself for doing so. How could such a question possibly sound anything other than idiotic, or even cruel?

'Well, I've been better, mate . . .' A dismissive wave of the hand. 'But there we are.' He laughed weakly. 'Although I suspect my dreams of competing in this year's Olympics may now be a tad unrealistic.'

Calvert, unable to think of anything more meaningful to say, settled for the obvious. 'Is there anything I can do for you, or get you? Anything, just say.'

Art looked him straight in the eye. 'Now you mention it, I wouldn't mind a new body—I've certainly buggered this one up.' He paused. 'Sorry . . . bit morbid. Maybe a week or two on a beach somewhere warm. Have heard Jamaica's nice this time of year. Mind you, I've always quite fancied Morocco too. Bugger it, the burden of choice can be such a bastard at times.'

Calvert smiled. This was a brief return to the Arthur O'Sullivan of old. 'I'll see what I can do.'

'Seriously though, mate, I'm okay. But it's obvious something's eating you . . . pretty sure I know what it is, but how much help I can be remains to be seen. Try me anyway.'

A little surprised at his friend's possible insight, Calvert shook his head in a gesture of despair. 'It's Elliot. Apparently he's gone off the rails a bit, got into this opioid stuff . . . you know, this Oblivion shit that's doing the rounds. To tell you the truth, I'm not really sure how to deal with it.'

Taking a gulp of tea, O'Sullivan frowned and scratched at his beard. 'Yes, I have to confess to you, I do know a little about this already. Kim did send me a message a couple of days ago. I haven't replied to it yet as I wanted to speak with you first.'

'She told you before *me*?' Calvert was unable to keep the hurt from his voice. 'I can't believe she'd do that.'

'Get past it, Marcus. I don't know her reasons and never asked, but maybe she just needed to talk to somebody not as emotionally attached as yourself. Like I say, I didn't ask.'

The two men stared at each other, both knowing the real reason but neither of them about to bring it up. Art tapped a finger on the table. 'Whatever, this isn't about you, me or even Kim, so let's just forget the *why*, and instead work out what you intend to do.'

Calvert shrugged, admitting to himself that, as was so often the case, Art was right. Now was not the time for self-pity.

'Let me be honest with you, Marcus, I don't know how you beat this, but obviously you need to start by talking to Elliot and getting his take on it before you can do anything at this point.'

'Since when has that made any difference? He hasn't wanted to listen to anything I've had to say for years.' Calvert took a gulp of tea and wondered how this could have happened. Why did his brain feel so numb, so dismally out of sync with everything around him? It was as though all the years of isolation had robbed him of the ability to deal with anything that wasn't simple day to day normality. Unable to come up with any plan of action, or even a worthwhile suggestion, he couldn't remember ever feeling more inadequate in his life.

Art dumped another spoonful of sugar into his tea and pointed in Calvert's direction with the spoon. 'Look, I'll tell you what I know about this crazy shit your boy is mixed up in. I'm not saying it's much, but if it helps, well . . .'

Not for the first time, Calvert wondered from what sources his friend obtained his knowledge—especially concerning things which were happening on the streets of a city he tended to avoid like the plague. He nodded limply. 'Okay, let's hear it."

The old man cleared his throat. 'This Opioid Oblivion stuff, Double O—whatever you want to call it—it's sold in the pleasure bars, okay? Supposedly illegal, but trust me, that's bullshit. I've not heard of anyone actually being busted for selling it, or even nabbed by the Snoopers using it openly on the street. So, yeah, I think it's safe to say it's most likely government-sanctioned and supplied.'

Calvert sat up straight, shaking his head. 'Not sure if I can believe that. Sounds a bit far-fetched to me.'

'You think? I wouldn't put *anything* past those bastards. I might be wrong . . .' Art shrugged. 'But then again, I've been right about far less likely things. I tell you, Marcus, very little of what you believe to be

91

true actually is. Most of everything you were ever taught at school is bollocks for a start. Not so much education—more like indoctrination.'

'Maybe, but it's still a big step to go from lying to people to destroying their health.'

'Really? The human race has been inflicting pain and suffering on each other for years. You, Marcus, go out there and murder someone and just watch the outrage. But those in power can send their armed forces to slaughter tens of thousands—millions, even—and for some reason it's considered different, often justifiable.'

Calvert was gagging for a cigarette. 'Yeah, I get what you're saying, but surely there are times when military intervention just can't be avoided—you know, the last resort.'

'Yeah, right.' O'Sullivan was having none of it. 'Have you ever questioned how, for example, every conflict we've involved ourselves in over the last hundred years or so is sold to us? Never as an invasion of another country to plunder its goodies, but rather to establish a necessary democracy, or some glorified liberation of an oppressed nation. However it starts or finishes, we're pictured as the all-conquering heroes—protectors of the globe. We overthrow murderous dictators on foreign soil, yet elect homegrown sociopaths of our own to bow down to and obey. Right from infancy we're programmed rather than taught, instructed to follow a path which we are told is the normal one to take, and therefore the correct one.'

From past experience, it was now obvious to Calvert that the conversation was rapidly nose-diving into one of Art's political rants, and further interruption would only serve to delay what he'd come here to discuss. Deciding to remain silent, he instead simply nodded his head and tried to look as though he was seriously absorbing what he was hearing.

'For example, when I was a kid, our books would typically portray a criminal as the stereotypical villain. You know, running around in a highwayman mask with a bag of swag over his shoulder, usually being chased down the street by a truncheon-wielding policeman. The law was, of course, always on the side of decency and justice whilst the criminal, obviously not.' Art stared at Calvert, a slightly manic glaze to his eyes as if daring him to challenge his theories. 'It takes years of life experience before you finally arrive at the correct conclusion that the two are not the polar opposites you were led to believe. In actual fact, they are usually entwined with one another—or even worse, one and the very same thing. Think about it for a minute. This bullshit is forced upon us as children by people who have already reached sufficient age and experience to know that what they are peddling is nothing but bollocks. So why then do they do it?'

Calvert just stared at him blankly, wondering if the old man was aware that, as usual, he'd taken the conversation somewhat off-track.

Without waiting for an answer, Art ploughed on. 'It's because they themselves are taught to, plain and simple. It's one generation feeding the next with history they know to be untrue, but are so locked in to this perpetual cycle of deceit, they carry on spouting it regardless. If you don't believe in God, you won't get into Heaven; you must scrub your face before meals; don't play with your dick—the list is bloody endless.' He noisily downed the remains of his tea, shifted position in his chair and was off again. 'But it's not just confined to childhood, that's just the beginning. From there, it not only continues, if anything it bloody escalates. Everyone becomes so absorbed in the day to day bullshit of scratching a living, they have neither the energy nor inclination to question the *bullshit* they're being fed. The thing is, it's not just—' he paused for breath. 'Look, what I'm trying to say, in my usual roundabout way, is that *anything* is a commodity to be sold for political gain, or simply just profit to the highest bidder regardless of who they are. Be it missiles, guns, information—even women and kids, for fuck's sake—it all has a price. Why do you think drugs would be any different? Believe me, if there's money to be made in anything, the bastards will exploit it.'

Calvert badly needed a drink, even more than he did a smoke. 'So basically there is nobody who can help, is that what you're saying?'

'Don't waste your time approaching the authorities, Marcus, you won't get any help or semblance of truth from any of them. Plus, you might just make matters worse.'

'So what do I do then, where do I go from here? I promised Kim I could sort this, but I honestly don't know if I can.'

O'Sullivan looked thoughtful for a moment, leaning forward, elbows on the table taking his weight. His voice was beginning to sound hoarse. 'Speak to your lad to start with. If he wants your help, at least you're halfway there.'

'And if he doesn't?'

Maneuvering himself back in his chair, the old man grimaced in the process. 'Let's not go there yet, mate. You might even find it's not as bad as Kim's made out, you know what she's like.'

Calvert would not be placated. 'Elliot of all people, I can't believe it. Why?'

'Not trying to be a dick here, Marcus, or downplay anything, but we're all addicted to *something* . . . me included. My medication, for example.'

'You can't really count medication. That's different, not really your choice, is it?'

'Choice doesn't always come into it—but okay, I'm addicted to being an awkward old bastard then, nobody can dispute that one.'

'True.' Calvert laughed for the first time that day. 'So what about Kim then—or Gideon, what's their addictions?'

Art nodded thoughtfully. 'Kim? Well, for a start, all those stupid bloody gizmos she keeps buying. The minute a new one comes onto the market, she has to have it—doesn't make a difference whether it's any good or not. It can be the most useless piece of crap imaginable . . . and usually is. As for Hurst, where the fuck do you start? Adulation, admiration, adoration—and that's just the A's—need I go on? Totally obsessed with his own self-importance. That has to count, surely?'

'Ha, I guess so. What about me then?'

'You're an odd fucker for sure, Marcus. Putting aside your terrible smoking habit, you are the rarest breed of all—probably the worst kind too. Like everyone else, you have your addictions, you just haven't recognised them yet . . . but on top of that, you are also a *reverse* addict. You automatically reject, rather than slowly absorb—not saying that's wrong, of course, but it can be equally self-damaging.'

'Wow, that's bloody profound, even by your standards.' Calvert laughed. 'That's me sussed.'

In the silence which followed, his thoughts soon returned to the situation at hand—one he felt less than qualified to deal with. 'Art, be honest with me, how serious do you think this stuff with Elliot really is?'

The old man was slow to reply. 'I really can't say, mate . . . let me talk to someone . . . see what I can find out for you.'

It was by now plainly obvious that Art had exhausted himself and was starting to wilt. As though too heavy for him to hold upright, his head nodded limply, repeatedly making its way down to his chest before being jerked upwards again. Calvert, lost in his own problems, had momentarily forgotten his friend's declining health—the disease which was slowly stealing away everything of the person he once was. Remembering too that he'd woken him just a half hour or so earlier, he was suddenly struck by feelings of self-reproach at his own thoughtlessness. Mindful that he hadn't visited for at least two weeks, he felt the guilt and shame of a man who, once again, was failing to step up to the mark. Somebody who had opted to take the easy option and keep his distance, to then turn up on a sick man's doorstep when it suited him, armed with his own troubles.

Rising from his chair, he made his way over to him and threw his arm around his shoulder, not sure whether it was meant as a gesture of comfort, or merely to appease his own conscience. 'Thanks for this, Art, it's been good to see you. I'll let you get some sleep now.'

Crossing the kitchen floor to leave, he turned to look back at his friend, but the old man no longer seemed aware of his presence. Instead, he was just staring straight ahead, his eyes fixated on something in the corner. Calvert followed his gaze to what looked like a chair, covered over with a white cotton sheet. At that moment it dawned on him, not only what it was, but also why he'd sensed something was different when he'd first arrived. Lowering his eyes, he hastily retraced his steps along the passage to the front door, before disappearing into the cold night, unable to rid his mind of the image of a wheelchair.

12

The hour was just inching its way past 10pm, and for Elliot Calvert, propped up against the bar in The Prism, the evening looked all set to be another typically uneventful one. Again he checked the time, noted that only six minutes had elapsed since he last looked, and calculated there was approximately another fifty-five to kill. For the want of something better to do, he raised his empty pint glass in a half-hearted endeavour to catch the barman's attention. It was his second attempt, and like his first, failed to get noticed. He wasn't concerned; he'd never been much of a drinker anyway, even less so when it was this bloody cold. Casting his eyes around the room's ochre-coloured perimeter, he searched for something more interesting than his own thoughts, but found little in the handful of diehards, who like himself, had chosen to brave the elements, and very likely for the same reason.

It was now nearly eight hours since his appointment at the AIR-Group tower, and so far a slight grogginess in his head was the only evident side effect from his earlier procedure. He wasn't sure exactly what had happened in the hour he'd been unconscious—if indeed anything at all. On waking, he was offered something to drink, allotted ten minutes to regain his senses, but told very little before being discharged.

In the weeks leading up to his appointment, he'd taken the time to read up on Random Thought Observation (or R.T.O. as it was more generally referred to) and been surprised at just how clandestine the subject appeared to be. Although by no means a new concept, like many other psychological experiments, it had for the most part been hidden behind a wall of secrecy. This was obviously something of a setback for anyone hoping to research it, but certainly not unusual, as information regarding anything that could be even remotely defined as 'sensitive' was limited. Still, picking through the bones of available facts and figures, he'd found enough to convince himself there was little to lose by at least giving it some consideration.

Originally a government-funded programme conceived sometime before the Dredge Wars, R.T.O. had been all set to become the future of warfare. With the ability to read a soldier's mind also came the understanding of their inner strengths and weaknesses, all of which could be honed (or more accurately, manipulated) to suit any agenda.

Although promising at first, progress over the years would be continuously hampered by bureaucracy, religious zealots and left-wing protest groups who branded the practice as unethical. This was to have little impact long-term, other than forcing the government to kick their PR machine into gear. A bureau was then established, whose sole purpose was to 'sweeten' the true nature of what they were engaged in and generally make it more palatable to the public. The official line then became that implementation of these procedures was not only necessary for the preservation of the soldier, but the end result would also serve as "a much valued contribution towards a safer society".

In the meantime, the mechanics of war changed entirely. No longer was it to be fought from trenches or in the skies, but instead on virtual battlefields, utilising stealth, sanctions and sabotage. If there was one thing the leaders of all nations could agree on, it was that, in the pursuit of wealth and power, too many precious reserves had been depleted. Modern day military conflicts could not be won, so consequently, they should not be fought. Obviously, the same age-old disagreements between countries would continue to arise, therefore alternative methods by which to settle them needed to be found. These were to take form in all manner of ways: from illicitly obtaining another's sensitive intelligence for the purpose of extortion or possible disclosure, to infiltrating and seizing control of their communications networks. Without rolling out one solitary tank or firing a single shot, through sheer cunning and inventiveness alone, any nation had the capacity to bring another to its knees. Not one country held the advantage; size was immaterial, as was colour or creed. Peace was maintained by mutual respect, along with the underlying fear that in threatening or exposing another, there was the strong possibility their own crimes could be revealed to the entire world.

However, the R.T.O. technology would not be abandoned. An undisclosed consortium of investors stepped forward and the research continued, albeit with a slight change in direction. Over the next few decades, thought patterns, dreams and memories were to become big business, largely due to the foresight of Elliot's own grandfather Valentine, and the technical abilities of his business partner Gideon Hurst. Through the highly-innovative program they had created—one which enabled thoughts and memories to be transferred to digital image—the success of the AIR-Group was as good as set in stone. When the pleasure bar craze exploded onto the scene four years ago, Hurst was quick to capitalise on it, becoming sole producer and distributor of all film material viewed in the booths. While it did still have its critics, it would seem that Random Thought Observation was, at least for the foreseeable future, here to stay.

In Elliot's opinion, the few pretty insignificant side effects he'd heard others speak of were greatly outweighed by the financial rewards. So, after much thinking, and assurances that it was a pain-free and harmless procedure, he had seized the opportunity and signed himself up. The card for the sum of one hundred and fifty denarii-dollars handed to him at the reception desk on his way out lay safely in his jacket pocket, but he knew it wouldn't be there long.

There were overdue payments on his tiny flat to pay, his recent discovery of the pleasure booths and Oblivion all but draining him of his miserable weekly wage.

On his walk back from the tower, Elliot had calculated that if he was to submit himself for observation once a week (the maximum attendance permitted), the extra income generated would more than cover his rent. Now, as his stomach rumbled, he was reminded that he hadn't eaten anything since the previous evening. Despite his lack of appetite, he promised himself he would grab something on his way home if only to keep his energy levels up. Next to him, his companion Seb muttered something incoherent, followed by a rather sapless whoop of delight. His face shone with sweat, bathed in the brilliant blue glow of a single flickering lens. The other was clear, temporarily switched off as was requested in a public building.

Seb was okay, could be a good laugh at times, but his enthusiasm for anything sports-related, especially Cyberball, was something Elliot would never understand. He watched him fidget and drool for a while, but it was obvious his friend was too engrossed in his game to be much company this evening.

'Oh well, looks like another shit Saturday night,' he sulked, shivering as the door opened and a sudden draught found him. 'I'm gonna do a booth, you up for it?'

Seb made no reply. Instead he just sat there on the edge of his stool, his fist beating against his knee, oblivious to everyone and everything, lost within the parameters of a little blue world which glimmered before his right eye.

'Suit yourself,' mumbled Elliot, reaching for his coat and heading for the dark and dingy back room, towards where his own predilection lay waiting.

The pleasure booths here were very much *no-frills* in design and numbered only four, whereas some of the more prestigious venues like The Orb and Vertigo were fitted out with at least a dozen or so. In Elliot's opinion, these larger and more corporate pleasure bars lacked atmosphere, and served merely as overpriced havens for the rich kids and posers. Instead he found himself gravitating towards the character and individuality of the smaller, more independent haunts.

Here, the booths themselves were no bigger than the usual toilet cubicles, and likewise, positioned side by side in a row. Nothing in their outward appearance revealed their true purpose; not one was distinguishable from another, save for a little white digit in their top right hand corner. All four of them were now more or less silent as he approached, except for a barely audible—yet still quite unpleasant—groaning from number one, the telltale trickle of blue light creeping out from around the edges of its door. Checking the others, Elliot found them to be currently not in use, so settled for number four, anxious to put as much distance between himself and the occupant of number one as possible.

Once inside the booth, he proceeded to make himself comfortable in the semi-reclined chair at the far end. About three feet away, fixed to the back of the door, the hologram screen stared back at him, black and lifeless, save for a thumbnail-size blue dot in its centre. To his left was an instruction panel, which like the screen, was presently in some kind of sleep mode. The only evident sign of life was a flashing V-shaped corporate logo above an illuminated square, requesting payment. Dropping his card onto it, Elliot leaned over towards the now-awakened panel; above his head the lights dimmed until they had reduced the room to the required darkness.

He studied the menu as he always did, clicking through the various categories—WAR. COMEDY. PORN.—and as usual, disregarded them all, trawling through until he came to his usual preference, strangely classified as SURREAL. This was a definition which to him made little sense—surely *all* the visuals shown in the pleasure booths were surreal by the very nature of their conception? How could anything extracted from the conscious or subconscious of the human brain be anything *but* surreal?

Regarding his choice of viewing material, Elliot had recently come to the conclusion that what he needed most was tranquility—anything which could assist in the soothing of his fragile and troubled psyche. Seb was hooked on the violent stuff but that wasn't for him; his dreams were disturbing enough without inviting more darkness in.

The fuzzy, multi-coloured images now drifted across the screen in their usual random and undefined manner, the hidden subliminal suggestions within them virtually undetectable amongst the chaos. He lay back and imagined he was travelling through the cosmos, happy to go wherever the journey happened to take him . . . to lose himself . . .

A flash of white, and for just a moment he felt himself disconnect from the film, reluctantly transported back to his grubby little cubicle and the futility of everything. He'd been miles away, for maybe no longer than ten minutes, but long enough to have reached a state of tranquility impossible to find anywhere other than inside these four flimsy walls. Maybe if he was to concentrate hard enough, he could fall back into it again, pick up from where he left off—*reconnect*? But he knew from experience the moment had passed; all that remained for him now was to make the most of the remaining booth-time he'd paid for.

The stream of visuals continued. However, by now he was struggling to keep his attention focused on them—or indeed anything other than the voice within his head and the delights of which it spoke. Before long, all other lines of thinking would crumble away, leaving only his desire for the Opioid Oblivion remaining. It wasn't until afterwards, in the cold light of day, that Elliot could see the dangers of the path he was being led down. But without it, what did he have? What was out there for the Elliot Calverts of the world to look forward to? Days spent locked in a soulless job, gathering consumer data for a company most likely not even aware of his existence? Or evenings sitting around in a poky ground floor apartment, gazing out over identical and similarly depressing, prefabricated hovels? His social life offered him little satisfaction and certainly no stimulation, each weekend nothing more than a mundane replica of the one which had preceded it.

On the screen, a cluster of grotesquely twisted trees were becoming engulfed in water, momentarily turning the booth a vivid hue of green before ebbing away to reveal a figure sleeping in a bed.

He'd often wondered if it was the same in every city. Although there were licenses available which granted you permission to travel, their acquisition was a tedious and complicated process. Elliot had never actually applied for one himself, but was once reliably informed by an older colleague at work that the screening you were subjected to in order to obtain one was excessive, and occasionally even humiliating. Not that he would ever have the funds required to leave Mother City and Sector 21, even for just one day. He'd long ago written that one off as nothing more than an unrealistic pipe dream.

Intelligent enough to know that opioids, especially ones as brutal as Oblivion, were not a long-term solution to all the tedium and drudgery in his life, Elliot had nonetheless weakened and succumbed to their calling. Having himself on occasion witnessed the carnage and misery they could so often leave in their wake, he was surprised at just how blasély he'd thrown caution to the wind and followed the trend. As always, he assured himself it was all under control—that his awareness of the potential danger would be what kept him from going the same way others had. If the time was to ever come when he found himself in over his head, he would be aware of it, and get the hell out.

Before him, the screen briefly dimmed as the colours drained away to be replaced by a foggy grey emptiness. From its centre, a pale daub began to grow, mutating until finally it was to assume the form of a gravestone. For a few seconds it hung there, warping and swelling, before splitting down the middle to open out like the centre pages of a book. There were written words but nothing that could be deciphered—or were they hieroglyphics? They shifted shape so rapidly, it was difficult to tell. He absently wondered what would be a fitting inscription on his *own* gravestone when the day came.

HERE LIES NOBODY WORTH REMEMBERING
DIED TRYING TO ESCAPE NORMALITY

The film ended abruptly, its final image being what appeared to be the twisted wreckage of old war machines covered in a blanket of snow. Then again, maybe that was just his interpretation?

As the lights crept back on, gradually making their way back to full brightness, the screen resumed its black nothingness. Now somewhat disoriented, Elliot raised himself from the chair, pocketed his card and stumbled through the booth door. Immediately outside, a stocky and rather unpleasant-looking man was hovering, waiting for it to become vacant. Wearing a blue pinstripe suit and a pained expression, he was careful to avoid eye contact, brushing impatiently past with a brusque ''scuse us,' instantly followed by the stale reek of cigarettes.

Returning to the bar, he looked around for Seb, before spotting him in the corner on the recently installed Space Razor machine. Leaning against it for support, he was lurching drunkenly from side to side as he punched the huge, bulbous buttons. The blue lens still glowed, but with a little less vibrancy than earlier. Elliot was about to tell him he was leaving and see if he wanted to tag along, before remembering the woman he was going to meet would not take kindly to him turning up with a stranger in tow. Instead, he checked the time and the denarii-dollar cash card in his jacket pocket. He'd better go. She didn't like to be kept waiting, and at times had been known to turn away custom if it wasn't on her terms. But first he needed something to lift his spirits, and luckily for him, he was in the right place to get it. Eight feet beneath the sticky, threadbare carpet on which he now stood, concealed deep within the cellar walls, a rather more unorthodox bar would already be coming to life—one which served not one morsel of food, nor a single drop of spirits or beer. In fact, the 'Poppy Drop' as it would affectionately come to be named, only ever had the one item on its menu. Not that this was of great concern to its clientele—himself included. As far as Elliot Calvert was concerned, variety was an overrated quality.

13

Calvert was fast losing hope that he might find something to occupy his restless mind. Midnight had come and gone and still he was unable to settle, let alone consider the possibility of grabbing a little sleep. Ever since returning from seeing Art a couple of hours previously, he'd more or less chain-smoked his way through the entire contents of his tobacco tin. He now mooched around his sitting room, back and forth like some caged animal, filling every corner with a blue fog. Having consumed close to a third of a bottle of scotch in the process, he could at last begin to feel the result. Telling himself it would have to be the last one, he poured another, before burying the bottle towards the back of the cupboard. Dragging a wooden chair over to the stove, he slumped himself down upon it to contemplate his next move. For the next few minutes he hardly stirred, his eyes fixed on the whisky tumbler in his hand. Through the haze which swirled inside his head, he now reached out to the one vestige of certainty still lingering there; he didn't know what, but he would have to do something.

His jacket still lay in the middle of the floor where he'd carelessly thrown it down earlier. Calvert now scooped it up, pausing only long enough to stuff his tobacco tin into a pocket before heading for the door.

Outside, the rawness of a 2am February morning hit him full-on, the biting wind taking him a little by surprise. Against a clear, starlit sky and unhindered by clouds, the full moon seemed almost ablaze, like some glorious celestial spotlight. To each side of the grey concrete path ahead, the two small white patches of hardened grass glittered, brought alive by its beam. But for once, its beauty was lost on Calvert as he looked around him, checking for signs of life—human or otherwise. With his shoulders hunched and his face lowered, he tucked his chin inside the top of his jacket and set off into the cold night.

Turning right out of Gatling Drive and rounding the corner, he looked towards Art's house, in his mind replaying their earlier conversation. Set back from the road, the whitewashed walls, now more of a ghostly grey, were just visible through the tall trees surrounding them, as was the kitchen window where a light still burned. Once again, the disappointment he felt in himself plucked at his conscience.

As he walked past the Harper's property, it dawned on him that he'd not seen either Jacob or Imogen Harper for several weeks. Struck by how uninhabited the place looked, he wondered whether something might have happened to them. Even the darkness could do little to hide the run-down appearance, instantly reminding him of Hurst's feeble bomb joke. Telling himself he would look into it, he added it to his mental to-do list, along with the still-pending dispatching of the Councillor's walking cane before its absence was noticed. A further visit from Gideon Hurst, should he decide to return for it, was not something Calvert needed right now. But something was definitely wrong here, that much was obvious. How had he failed to notice before now? He'd walked by the house enough times recently, usually in broad daylight too. How could he have been so distracted?

Drawing on his cigarette, he realised it had died between his fingers. Steadying himself against the Harpers' gatepost, he fumbled around in a pocket for his lighter. Close by, a dog began to howl, a long and drawn-out cry—one startling enough to cause him to look up. It was then he first noticed what it might be that was causing the animal's distress. In the distance, hovering a few feet above the road's surface, a small red light moved slowly through the darkness towards him, its approach smooth and level—purposeful. Not once did it stop or deviate from its trajectory, the tarmac before it no longer black, but rather a sinister shade of crimson. Any remaining doubt as to the source of the light now evaporated, taking his courage with it.

Although in itself not that unusual, the sighting of an M.S.O. anywhere outside the city zones was generally construed as an ominous sign. There would certainly be a reason for it being here now, other than merely a routine patrol. For a brief moment he entertained thoughts of escape, before dismissing them as sheer lunacy. Fleeing and hiding was no longer a viable option—no, his best course was simply to stand still and not antagonise it in any way.

Nearer . . . nearer . . . nearer . . .

As though rooted to the spot, Calvert could do little more than watch as the Snooper closed in, knowing that with every passing second, his options were becoming fewer—the silent distance between the two of them shorter . . . *shorter . . . nearer.*

As the Snooper drew level, something slammed into his shoulder, the impact enough to send him staggering back into the Harpers' fence. Instinctively he reached a hand up, certain of the open wound he would find there, but his fingers found only a burning sensation, nothing more. Now within just a few feet of where he was standing, it rose up before him, twisting and flexing like some grotesque metal serpent preparing to strike. Beneath its fiery red glare, Calvert braced himself for the second blow, but it never came. Instead, the M.S.O.'s grey metal skull began to slowly descend, until finally it was at eye-level, where it hung, motionless and menacing. Now merely an arm's length from his face, he could feel it crawling around inside him, filling every cell with heat—with pain. So invasive was the single optic beam that, even with his eyes screwed tightly shut, he was unable to prevent it from boring its way in. Outraged, he cried out for it to stop, tried to reason with the machine, but his words were reduced to little more than pathetic rasps. He wondered how close he was to passing out, aware that to be rendered unconscious on a night like this would mean certain death from hypothermia. It didn't make sense. What possible motive could it have for attacking him in the first place? He'd done nothing wrong, or provoked it in any way. And who would have authorised its presence here—more to the point, why?

And then, without any warning or apparent reason, the Snooper released its hold on him, gradually easing itself backwards until enough ground had been crossed to suggest it was leaving. Surrounded by hazy pools of red light, it crept further and further into the distance, before coming to a halt about a hundred feet away, where it seemed to have a sudden change of plan. Calvert now watched in dismay as it began to return, this time weaving across the tarmac in an erratic zig-zag motion until once again it was level with him. For about ten seconds it did nothing more than just stare at him, only moving away to repeat the exact same manoeuvre.

Reverse—wait—forward—intimidating pause. This bizarre display of superiority continued, over and over again, until eventually the hideous contraption seemed to tire of the game. Without further torment, it spun around and accelerated away, its turret eye rotating as it peered down pathways for anything which could be possibly classified as suspicious activity. Calvert watched until he could see it no more, fearful that at any moment it might reappear to carry on where it had left off.

After a few minutes, he could feel his senses beginning to revert back to normal, any previous feelings of terror diminishing, to be replaced by those of extreme cold. Touching his face, he was surprised to find it wet with perspiration; he would have to get moving before his body temperature plummeted. With trembling fingers, he withdrew his tobacco tin and set about rolling himself a cigarette from the dregs, wishing he'd had the forethought to knock up a supply of them before leaving the house. Turning to shelter the lighter's flame from the wind, he drew deeply on the roll-up, the nicotine gradually calming him as the adrenaline in his system began to recede. Throwing the butt down to the tarmac, he ground it to nothing beneath his boot as he contemplated what to do. Common sense was telling him to return home, yet his ingrained obstinance would not allow it. Once again Calvert set off, his progress slightly impeded by the constant stopping to check behind him.

Before long, he'd left Gunners Park, turning right to head down Pilgrims Hill, the long and unlit road which would eventually lead into the city. Still a little shaken by the incident with the Snooper, he was already craving another cigarette, yet reluctant to remove his chilled hands from the jacket's pockets, despite the thin leather offering them little refuge from the cold air. A hover-shuttle sped past in the opposite direction, its soft purr only audible in the few seconds before it reached him. Somebody riding it shouted something as it passed by, followed by a shriek of drunken laughter. But their words were lost to him, carried into the distance by the wind.

Twenty minutes later, he emerged from the darkness of Pilgrims Hill to be met with the glaring white light of the Outer Zones. For the third time that week, he was about to enter Mother City.

For as far as the eye could see, hideous industrial architecture thrust itself arrogantly towards the skies, both dominating and desecrating a once beautiful horizon with a fusion of smoke and steel. Calvert pictured the scenes within, the legions of disposable worker ants, all striving for even a miniscule taste of what their masters would have long taken for granted. Eagerly, they would be grabbing up any overtime on offer, in order to pay for the homes they would inevitably get to spend so little time in, alongside their children who they would inevitably spend so little time *with*. An invisible army trapped on treadmills of debt, foot soldiers prematurely burning themselves out before heading off to their graves, only to be replaced by younger, stronger—more compliant versions. It didn't escape Calvert that, if not for his inheritance, he too would be entombed in one of these units, watching the clock, counting down the days until the weekend.

It was hard to believe so much had changed, and so rapidly. The soft red brick of elegant Victorian housing, long torn down and erased from history, only to be replaced by concrete, plastic and vast acres of tinted glass, all in the name of progress and profit. Not that he necessarily disapproved of those who successfully built empires, but surely the wealth accumulated as a result could be put to a better purpose than simply using it to acquire more?

From somewhere deep inside the bowels of the faceless façade, a klaxon called out. *Tea break—End of tea break—Cigarette break—End of cigarette break—Shit break—End of shit break.* A summoning for someone or something, no doubt. Whatever, its cry was a command, and one which would undoubtedly be obeyed.

The horn's screech immediately transported him back to his first ever visit to the circus, something he hadn't thought about in a long while, despite it having been so significant to him at the time. A clown with long red hair pulled back from a huge white forehead had circled the arena in a little yellow car, periodically blasting one of these things as he went round. The noise was like nothing Calvert had ever heard, and all the acts that went before were instantly forgotten. Praying the car would be near him when it next sounded, just so he could hear it at full volume, he'd known then and there that he would have to have one of his own. It was his ninth birthday, and despite assurances from his father that as soon as his work was finished he would be joining both Calvert and his mother there, he had—as was par for the course—failed to materialise. So, once again, it was just the two of them, and to be honest, he wasn't unduly concerned at the time. Never having been to a real circus before, his excitement had been growing steadily as he counted down the days leading up to it. Nothing, not even the failure of his father to show up, could cast a shadow over the experience. Well, not for him, anyway.

Later that evening, after he'd gone to bed, there were raised voices through the walls—exchanges which were hard to decipher, but unmistakably angry. Without so much as an interlude, this war of words was to continue relentlessly into the night. Lying there unable to sleep, although a little afraid of the tension, Calvert had also felt a little excited by it too.

When he'd come down for breakfast the following morning, he was surprised to find his mother asleep on the couch, still fully clothed, with her big fur coat draped across her. On the sitting-room table lay some money on a plate like some generous tip left for a waiter. It was a present from his father, much the same as the one the year before. That day he didn't attend school; there was a klaxon and some other bits for his bike to be bought, and the thought of a six hour wait to get them was too much for him to endure. But that evening, nothing would be mentioned about their outing to the circus, nor anytime after. It was almost as though they had never been. This was the first time he'd thought about it in years.

Just then, a GlydeMaster swept around the corner towards him, its pleasant burble instantly recognisable. At first, thinking it might be Hurst and Deeks (or maybe Deeks on his own, partaking in some illicit joyriding), he slunk into the shadows, before noting the hover-car was not black, but pale in colour.

Calvert calculated he was now only about twenty minutes from where Elliot lived. He'd only ever been there twice, and not been overly impressed by what his son called home. A shoddily-built flat situated within a poorly-maintained complex, on what was generally accepted as being the least desirable part of the city. Once an attractive suburb, it was now difficult to imagine it as anything other than the over-developed eyesore it was gradually mutating into.

His initial instinct had been to head over there, talk things out with him, maybe even discover Kim was over-dramatising the situation—or better still, completely misreading it as Art had suggested might be the case. For the first time since leaving his house, Calvert could now see it was a mission which could only end in disaster. What did he think he could possibly achieve turning up there at this late hour, agitated and the worse for drink, preaching the evils of drug use? Especially when, as a parent, he'd done so little over the years to guide and educate his son—what sort of reception could he really expect? Turning around, he instead began to head in the opposite direction, thankful that once again common sense had prevailed. Removing his hands from his pockets, he cupped them to his mouth, breathing heavily upon his fingers until there was enough life in them to begin the task of rolling a cigarette. His pace quickened, some of the tension he'd been carrying in his shoulders easing slightly. He knew where he was going.

What wasn't so clear to him was *why?*

14

AutoButler v.3.1.7 - The AIR-Group Pat. No. 84828723 - Assignment GH-22

Update check *– update 376 rev6 found – applying firmware patch – firmware patch successful*

Client log *no. 9507e - Scan no. 6248*

Body temp. check/*abnormal/increased* - **Pulse rate check**/*abnormal/increased* - **Blood pressure check**/*abnormal/increased* *– high scan priority – close observation mode engaged*

**Environment/stimulus program changed/
high-active monitor 24 hrs/ initiate intervention/**

Scanning the never-ending list of cybernetic duties for the following day, the AutoButler noted that yet again there was no early morning alarm call included on the itinerary. For itself, this would mean valuable hours relief from the Councillor's constant bombardment of demands—time which could be utilised recalibrating itself in Semi-Sleep Mode, or installing any new software which might have become available within the last twenty-four hours. Switching into Decipher Mode, it began the execution of one of its more laborious tasks: analysing and logging data. Once again it examined the results, vigilantly searching for any discrepancies—the minutest detail it could have overlooked. As expected, there were none. However, the entire compendium would have to be thoroughly re-examined before the Councillor awoke, whenever that happened to be.

The motionless figure on the couch, although still pale, was registering normal sleep patterns, having slipped into REM ten minutes prior. The AutoButler debated enabling Dream-Scan Mode, before reaching the conclusion it might be considered a breach of Machine Ethical Code, especially now that normal breathing had resumed and vital signs were finally beginning to stabilise. Instead, it calculated the conditions of the room, carefully adjusting heat and humidity to coordinate with the man's body temperature, which was still registering an unhealthy—yet not critical—low of 35.3°C since his recent session in the chair. Although not as disturbing as the previous night's episode, it was nonetheless evident that these incidents were still on the increase.

Over the weeks, the Councillor's (admittedly sparse) social life had become virtually non-existent, his behavior unpredictable, and at times even volatile. Even his personal grooming routine, once so important to him—almost to the point of being obsessive—was beginning to suffer. On some days it would appear to have been abandoned entirely. But above everything else, it was his poor level of sleep which was the greatest cause for concern to the AutoButler. For the most part it was fitful and sporadic, offering him little chance of regeneration, while the fluctuation of his respiratory rate demanded continual supervision. The optional Night Watchman Mode which had been activated several months back now seemed a permanent setting, during which the constant adjustments to the heating and air conditioning systems left the AutoButler little opportunity to focus on upgrading its own algorithms.

Often, the Councillor could be monitored wandering around the apartment in the early hours of the morning, mumbling to himself, his mind very obviously somewhere that was causing him distress. At other times, without warning he would suddenly erupt into outbursts of rage, his language foul and very much out of character. Above him, nestled amongst a plethora of transistors, multiple hard drives, and miles of copper data cable, the AutoButler duly noted and documented everything with typical diligence and competence. Under its watchful eye, nothing would go unseen or be left to chance, and no task within its capabilities was ever undertaken with anything less than one hundred percent efficiency. Undeterred by the Councillor's apparent lack of appetite, it had carried on making his meals, regardless of the fact that they remained largely untouched. Unsurprisingly, his weight had decreased significantly, falling by over four pounds during the course of a week. Music, carefully selected for the purpose of bringing him comfort, would be instantly snapped off to be replaced by a dark and brooding silence, during which he would just lie there, staring into nothing. Data also revealed significant dehydration and a general decline in cognitive capability. The deterioration of the Councillor's well-being was by now clearly evident, as was the disruption to his working day.

Always a stickler for punctuality, he would—until recently—have normally risen from his bed at 6:30am on the dot. After breakfast, which consisted of two vitamin pills washed down with a small cup of thick, oily coffee, he would then leave the apartment at 7:15 in order to arrive at the AIR-Group fifteen minutes later. It was a rare occasion to see him return any time before 6:30pm at the earliest.

Here also, the changes were all too apparent. Only two days during the previous week had seen the Councillor actually comply with this self-imposed ritual. On two others he would not be collected by his chauffeur until long after 11am, and on the Friday just gone he'd done very little for most of the day, choosing to spend it reclined on the sofa, either barking out orders or sleeping.

None of this would escape the scrutiny of the AutoButler. It was all on file for comparison, duly noted down in a subcategory of its own making, one which had been designated the classification 'Behavioural Abnormalities.'

A subcategory that seemed to be growing by the day.

15

When the dream came, it played through to the same part it always did before releasing him. Pulling the covers back around his chilled body, he breathed deeply and tried to focus his mind on anything other than the images which had jerked him awake. Inevitably, the details would vary slightly on each occasion, but not so the theme—*that* was to remain unchanged, predictable from being repeated over and over again for the last thirty years.

Even before his illness began to take hold, Art O'Sullivan was never the best of sleepers, and Calvert's visit had drained him of his precious few reserves. Now lying there, eyes wide open, he realised he had no recollection of even getting into bed. Turning to look towards the thin, russet-coloured curtains, he noticed the first signs of dawn beginning to creep through them.

This was the first winter to see him confined to his house. Until a couple of months ago he would always have been up and about by now, standing outside with his mug of sweet coffee to watch the sun rise. The bitterness of even the coldest day made little difference to him; it was one of his habits, and had been since he retired nearly eight years before.

It wasn't even as though he'd been consciously thinking about the face—he hadn't done so for quite a while—so why should it have returned now? Days and sometimes even weeks could pass without it coming to him, but he knew it would never leave for good. Hidden just beneath the surface of his thoughts, it would lurk in the darkest recesses of his mind, biding its time, as it waited for his subconscious to reel it back in.

And why was it all so lucid still? How was it that three decades could not even begin to diminish the true horror of what he'd stumbled upon that evening? At least then it might have offered him *some* relief, possibly even allowed a little doubt to slip in—just a glimmer of hope that somehow it hadn't been as abhorrent as his memory had led him to believe. By now, the hideous visage was as familiar to him as his own face, almost as though they had become one entity. As clearly defined as any one of the pictures which hung on his sitting-room wall, every last gruesome detail would remain mercilessly intact: its gossamer-thin skin, the colour of greaseproof paper and with a similar translucency; the broken, misshapen nose; the bloodless lips practically eclipsed by the dark stubble surrounding them. But it was the eyes which really haunted him. Those dead fish eyes that stared back at him, vacuous and milky. They would always be there, permanently etched into his memory.

Even to this day, Art couldn't honestly say whether the man had actually been alive or dead, but something inside him told him it was neither—maybe even both. Was there a difference? Whatever, he'd carried it around in his head ever since.

His thoughts automatically reverted back to that unforgettable encounter, the one and only time he was to actually see it for real. In total, the entire incident could not have lasted any longer than twenty seconds. It was, however, twenty seconds which would change the rest of his life.

He often found it strange that in later years he could remember everything so clearly; on the night in question, it was all just a blur. A couple of minutes either way, and for him it would have never happened.

In 2028, Art O'Sullivan had been chief supervisor of construction within the AIR-Group. As one of the original five, his role was a pivotal one—possibly more than would be credited to him at the time. However, to those who understood such things, there was little doubt that without his input, the innovative brainchild of Valentine Calvert and Gideon Hurst was unlikely to have been given its gift of life. His vast knowledge of engineering had been critical for the design and fabrication of the massive aluminium tower, and an impressive track record in the heavy construction industry had seen him short-listed. But ultimately, it would be his friendship with Valentine which would clinch the deal.

The only one of its kind in Mother City—or anywhere for that matter—the tower was as radical as it was impressive, its purpose both controversial and intriguing. Although he would later distance himself from the project, there could be no denying that it was responsible for many of the opportunities that had come his way in the era which followed. Whatever O'Sullivan's personal feelings, the strange-looking edifice would be viewed as a measure of his architectural prowess by contractors and industrialists alike. In addition to being paid handsomely for his services, he'd also gained much recognition and respect from his peers, and from that point onwards, his name would be forever synonymous with monolithic design and development.

Yet something about the project in general would never truly feel a hundred percent ethical to him. The fact that the funding was to come not from the government as he'd initially been led to believe, but rather in the form of a donation from an undisclosed source, was in itself a little suspicious. Even more so was Valentine's decision to wait until many months after construction had commenced before admitting to this fact, and even then it was with some degree of reticence. Choosing not to reveal the identities of the mystery benefactors, he did however let slip that they were a consortium of oligarchs known as The Suzerain.

Here was where the lines first started to become a little blurred, the point where Art would begin to sense something a little *cloak and dagger* concerning the operation he was involved in. Regardless, he'd pushed any doubts aside, reminding himself that much like the areas of research the AIR-Group were to embark on, any financial matters were not his concern. The whole concept of monitoring and recording the subconscious mind was a complex one, not to mention a contentious subject, and very much outside his own field of expertise.

It had been just over two years since the conception of the company, and already it had expanded further. With the structure of the tower concluded, plans for a further laboratory on the other side of the city were drawn up in readiness. This new development would once again be bankrolled from the shadows, and like before, be under Art's control. From locating a suitable site to liaising with architects, developers and contractors, it would ultimately be his project, and his alone for the majority of 2028. In actual fact, the whole scheme was completed ahead of schedule, with him triumphantly heading back to the AIR-Group headquarters towards the end of November, mission completed. A couple of weeks later, the incident which was to change his life would occur.

Returning to the tower late on that particular evening hadn't been his intention, but in his hasty departure earlier, he'd forgotten to pick up a replacement Slumber Nugget from the store. Ever the insomniac, over the previous months, Art was to find himself unable to sleep without one of these devices by his side. About the size and shape of a domino, it was another of Hurst's many inventions, and one of the company's top-selling products. Held against the forehead, the Slumber Nugget would pick up the negative vibrations that were preventing sleep from occurring, then isolate and remove them. Completely safe and painless, the results were immediate. Consequently, the user would awake the next morning, refreshed and clear-headed, to find the device lying on the pillow beside them. All very good, but Art's had failed the night before and a replacement was critical if he was to function the next day.

All was quiet as he'd walked up to the main doors of the tower, placed the palm of his hand upon a small glass panel and waited for the fingerprint scan to run its course. Stepping into the half-light of the reception area, he'd then proceeded along the corridor towards the rear of the building to where the store rooms were situated. It was as he was passing the doors to the lift, used primarily by staff to gain access to Level Two, that he became aware of the flashing green light, an indication that the elevator was descending.

Located at the tower's highest point, Level Two was pretty much a prohibited area to all but a select handful of AIR-Group personnel, and as far as Art was aware, should have been sealed up over an hour ago. Curious as to who could still be in the building and why they would be working so late, he'd hung about and waited for the doors to open.

A couple of minutes passed and still they remained closed, leading him to the conclusion that something must have malfunctioned. Stepping forward, he pressed his thumb repeatedly to the emergency-opening button until eventually the light switched to red. As the doors slid open, he immediately felt himself recoil, and instinctively backed away. Inside the lift, upon a hospital gurney, lay what could only be a person, covered from head to feet in a white sheet. Suspecting he might be caught up in the middle of some prank, Art had quickly recovered himself, and with a sly grin on his face, quietly stepped inside. Standing beside the gurney, he waited for about thirty seconds before taking hold of one corner of the sheet, whisking it away in the manner of a stage magician. 'Voila!' he cried out in triumph, a split second before reality hit him and the vomit began to rise in his throat. On the point of retching, he turned his head away, but against his better judgement stood firm. Placing a hand over his mouth, he reluctantly forced his eyes to return to the mutilated face which would go on to haunt his dreams for years to come.

A grotesquely misshapen cranium, larger than could be considered normal, exhibited bruises of all colours—a clear indication of them having been inflicted over a period of time. Incisions, dark and swollen, crossed the vertex like the jagged lines on a map, carelessly and crudely stitched back together with coarse black thread. The body was clothed in beige overalls bearing an embroidered emblem on one breast pocket, while on the other, the numerals *57823* were barely visible in faded black print upon a white label. It was a prison number. Stunned, Art staggered backwards out of the lift and into the corridor, where he slumped down, leaning against the wall opposite.

For over an hour he stayed there, smoking cigarette after cigarette, processing the implications of what he'd just witnessed. One thing was a certainty—he couldn't just pretend he hadn't seen it. He was also very aware that going in search of technicians for answers was pointless; there was little doubt this was something which went all the way to the top. Figuring there was little else he could do for the moment, he'd left a message for Valentine and then headed home to endure a fitful night—one made all the worse by the fact that he'd forgotten to pick up the Slumber Nugget, ironically the very reason for his having been there in the first place.

The next day, both Gideon and Valentine were keen to play down the incident—especially Valentine, who'd very likely spent most of the morning up until Art's arrival fabricating an explanation. Behind his leather-topped desk, reclining in his huge chair, he wore a look of indifference as he set about justifying the episode. Apparently, the man in the elevator was a life-serving convict who, for the sake of posterity, had volunteered to have his memories monitored and recorded. This was being conducted as part of an experimental insight into the workings of the criminal mind, and nothing more. When Art attempted to push him further on the subject, Valentine was quick to remind him that it was not his business to question either the areas of research or the ethics the AIR-Group happened to be engaged in. He then proceeded to emphasise that what they'd just discussed was obviously classified information, and as such, any mention of it to another person would be regarded as a breach of security. The scene which followed had turned ugly, finally becoming physical. Within the hour, Art O'Sullivan was gone.

He never officially resigned from his position, nor was he fired, but it was apparent to all parties concerned that his place in the AIR-Group was no longer tenable. There would be no attempt at reconciliation or even contact during the months which followed, from either party.

Since that fateful final meeting, Art had never spoken of the matter to anyone, not even Marcus. As far as he was concerned, it was buried in his past, along with the friendship he'd once shared with Valentine Calvert.

16

If not for the fullness of the moon, the tower would have been all but lost against the blue-black of the night sky. Rising from the ground not upright, but at an angle, even the shadows it cast were unique. Shamelessly unorthodox in appearance, it clearly had no intention of merely blending in. As though staking its claim amongst the surrounding nondescript architecture, it stood imperious and defiant, creating the illusion of something that had just thrust its way through the concrete.

Surrounding the base, fingers of iron reached out to support it like the rampant and gnarled roots of an ancient tree, not one the same as another in their configuration. As it climbed through the cold and brooding silence, it curved and narrowed towards its summit like some massive, metal phallus. Located approximately a third of the way up, on the end of what appeared to be some kind of offshoot limb, was the first of the two circular chambers, the second being located at the tower's pinnacle. Whilst Level One was relatively easy to see from the street below, Level Two was not. Due to the tower's height, it could only be made out in any detail from the windows of the city's tallest buildings. However, Art had once confirmed to Calvert that the two compartments were identical in both size and shape. Like the rest of the structure, these too were a dull grey in colour, their perimeters surrounded by a single row of oval windows from which, as night fell, an insipid yellow light would emerge.

Calvert stared up at it, allowing himself to become soothed by the gentle current of energy which seemed to radiate from somewhere within its walls. Relaxing his mind, he also discovered he could hear (or rather feel) the strains of music. Although faint, it was deceptively hypnotic, and soon he was lost amongst the eccentricity of its melodies, indulging himself in the brief respite it offered him from his troubles. Inserting his fingers into his ears he realised made no difference; the symphony remained there inside his head, eerie and strangely evocative. Eventually he discovered he had the ability to block it out with thought if he wished to, and reluctantly did so.

He wondered why he felt no sense of pride, or any form of attachment looking at the AIR-Group tower. It was, after all, the joint creation of his father and Hurst—the Calvert family legacy. Surely it should stir something in him?

During the many moments spent dwelling on, and attempting to make sense of his past, he'd become painfully aware that his father didn't actually feature there much at all. In fact, as a child growing up, Calvert had rarely seen him, and in time, would come to not just expect it, but to accept it also. Valentine Calvert's life was his work, whether it was doing research for the government before and during the Dredge Wars, or building his personal empire afterwards. Even back then, this wasn't something which would unduly trouble him, as the rare occasions they did spend in each other's company were usually lacking in both affection and attention. Right or wrong didn't come into it; it was their version of normality, and would no doubt have continued in much the same manner, had Valentine not suddenly disappeared.

Not for the first time, he now found himself considering the possibility that Elliot might feel the same level of disappointment he himself was later to become consumed by. Desperately, he now began to trawl back through his mind, searching for long forgotten fragments of their limited time spent together. The Pod Tower—that was it, the name they'd christened the beast he now stood before. From out of nowhere, a vague recollection reached out to him, bringing with it a sense of nostalgia and maybe a little hope too. For a moment he fought to recall the stories he'd told Elliot so long ago, as they passed by this very spot on their way home from school. It was no use, there was nothing; not one clear memory he could grab hold of in the attempt of reliving it.

Sadly, the only conclusion he could draw from this was that, as with his own father, moments spent with his son had maybe not been as precious to him as they should have been. Valentine's neglect of him, however, would have been the consequence of a fanatical ambition, whereas his own failings—although due partially to circumstance—had largely been brought on by apathy. As Calvert now stood there firing questions at himself, one in particular bothered him more than the others: by comparison, were his own failings *worse* than those of his father?

In truth, he'd found the role of being a parent far more tiring than he'd ever previously imagined it could be. The sleepless nights were to leave him feeling wrung out and irritable during the day, the sapped energy impossible to reclaim. Even when baby Elliot slept well, he himself could never quite manage to switch off, knowing that any minute he might awaken, crying to be fed. It was then he would feel resentful of Kim, lying next to him, dead to the world, her breathing deep and regular.

He'd often since questioned whether, at the time, she was ever fully aware of the turmoil building up within him—but then again, even if she had been, would it have made any difference in the end? It wasn't as though he'd never wanted to discuss his thoughts and emotions with her, so much as it being a level which for some reason they were unable to connect on. On the one occasion he'd finally plucked up the courage to bare his soul, she just looked at him flatly, shook her head in a dismissive fashion, and hastily changed the subject. It was not something he would repeat.

It had never been Calvert's wish for them to split up, but in the end, he simply resigned himself to what he'd come to regard as a ticking time-bomb. With Kim not prepared to carry on living at Gunners Park, and his point-blank refusal to even consider moving to Mother City, it was eventually to become something of a Mexican standoff.

Even to this day, there'd never been any doubt in his mind that her decision to leave would have been influenced by her newly-acquired friends—a clique of young and impressionable pseudo-intellectuals, who she would refer to as her "city homies". Largely made up from people Calvert had little in common with, and even less time for, he would do his utmost to avoid their company whenever possible. Unable to appreciate either their political views or juvenile humour, he'd been secretly pleased when Art was also to take an instant dislike to the group, later referring to them as "an appalling cluster of superficial, attention-seeking bores."

Although his summary may have been a little harsh, there could be no denying the elements of truth attached to it. If they weren't droning on about what stimulating social lives they were leading within the Inner Zones, or bragging inanely about some recent acquisition, they would endlessly yammer on about who or whatever happened to be in fashion that particular month. Even worse was their constant extolling of the virtues inner-city technology offered, such as microsecond download speed, and of course, the superior air quality.

Many years ago at a party, inebriated, bored and feeling a little antagonistic, he'd deliberately steered himself into an argument with a loud and particularly obnoxious guy called Tarquin. Tarks—as he insisted on being called—had found it necessary to paraphrase the government's claim regarding the purity of the oxygen inside the city's perimeter. For Calvert, who'd long held suspicions that the air was no different in Mother City than in the more rural areas such as Gunners Park or the ill-fated Callingden, it was a red rag to a bull. His counter-argument, however, was met with not only condescending rebuttals, but also derision. It hadn't helped the situation that he already considered Tarquin to be something of a sarky little prick, an observation he'd decided needed to be put forward then and there. The conversation was to deteriorate only further from that point onwards. Later that evening, back at home, Kim had rounded on him, suggesting that in the future he would do well to "leave his ridiculous opinions at home." Deciding to go one better, the next time a social gathering occurred, Calvert did indeed leave not just his opinions at home, but *himself* there also. It wasn't a long-term solution.

Now, looking at the tower again, with its peculiar, almost sinister design, he found himself questioning what sort of a man his father would really have been. A brilliant one, according to Gideon Hurst, but his was not a viewpoint Calvert especially valued. In Hurst's eyes, Valentine Calvert was without flaw. So great was the Councillor's admiration for his ex-partner's work that he would be blind to any of Valentine's parental failings.

The only other person with possible answers was Art O'Sullivan, and so far, he refused to be drawn on the subject. The few times Calvert had pushed him, it would quickly become obvious he was holding back, in particular with regards to the mystery surrounding his father's disappearance. In the end, he'd given up asking, surmising that Art either genuinely didn't know anything, or if he did, he was not about to divulge. However frustrating it was for him, he'd long decided that for the sake of their friendship he would leave it right there. But Valentine and Art *were* close once, that much was fact. Looking back, he could clearly remember the two of them often being in each other's company, up until a year or so before his father had vanished. Going back even further, he could recall Gideon Hurst also being present on occasion, but that was to become less frequent as time went by.

Calvert was just fifteen years of age when it happened. There had been no goodbyes or explanations, no note left—nothing. On the day in question, his father set off for work like he did on every other day, and that was the last anyone would see or hear from him. At the time, there was much speculation as to his whereabouts, especially at school where a certain group of kids were to take great delight in coming up with new theories to pass between themselves. But even that didn't compare with the hushed voices and sideways glances from so-called friends as he rounded a corner, or the deathly silence which would inevitably follow him into a classroom. Whether it was words of sympathy delivered through the patronising smiles of teachers, or simply puerile sniggers from the class dickhead, it seemed they'd all felt compelled to contribute in some way or other.

But it wasn't just confined to school. Amongst the adults, rumours of fraud and embezzlement were quick to circulate, despite a statement issued from the AIR-Group to the contrary. The official line was simply 'Valentine Calvert's whereabouts are presently unknown, as is any probable reason for his sudden absence.'

The weeks which followed had been miserable, but gradually some semblance of normality would begin to return to his life. But sadly, it would not be the same story for his mother, who'd become bitter and morose. For Ruth Calvert, this was to be the beginning of a downward spiral from which she would not recover. Never the most emotionally-stable woman even on her better days, she'd turned to drink to fill the void left by her husband. With her son rapidly approaching sixteen years of age and beginning to gain his independence, her fear that he too might drift out of her life had grown to irrational proportions, seeming to draw her ever further into a state of daily intoxication. With them both having been left well provided for, she'd found herself freed from the restraints of having to work for a living. But this newly-acquired liberation brought with it too many days which, for her, were empty of both purpose and pleasure. Two years after losing his father, Calvert watched his mother eventually succumb to cirrhosis of the liver. He'd recently turned eighteen and was, for the first time in his life, all alone in the world.

The months dragged by, and he had found himself beginning to hate the large city apartment. It was as if any little warmth or soul it might have once possessed were now sucked from it, leaving him nowhere to find solace. All that remained in the aftermath were the very memories he constantly sought to extinguish from his thoughts—a day to day reminder of a life he no longer had, and the people who were no longer there to share it with. Despite its considerable size, the house was beginning to feel claustrophobic to him, and before the year was out, he'd sold it. He then turned his back on Mother City.

With the proceeds from the sale, he'd instead chosen to purchase one of the vacant units on the Gunners Park Industrial Estate. Although requiring much renovation, it did have the benefit of being just around the corner from Art, the one person he felt the need to be near to.

Along with Callingden and Thornton Hamlet, Gunners Park was located beyond the Outer Zones of the city, pretty much as far out as it was possible to get without straying into the surrounding forests and overgrown fields. These were the last of the undeveloped areas of Sector 21, as yet unmolested by the developers and property magnates, cut off from the pulsating electrical currents which flowed through the veins of the city. Here, Calvert's broken spirit would gradually heal, and under the watchful eye of Art O'Sullivan, he'd applied himself to the task of transforming the unit into a small but decent four-room dwelling.

Number 7 Gatling Drive might have been a far cry from the grandeur of its predecessor, but nevertheless it was somewhere that brought him a sense of calm, something which for too long had been absent in his life.

And then along came Kim Lorna Maddox.

The Maddox family lived barely a stone's throw away, in a large but unfinished assortment of what was actually five or six micro units, all linked together by corridors. Their garden was by far the largest on the estate, and home to some bizarre metal sculptures, as well as an

131

interesting gathering of ancient and long-forgotten automobiles, their rusting shells all but hidden by brambles and foliage. It was soon obvious to him that both Brian and Mary Maddox were eccentric in that comical and endearing way you can't help but be drawn to. What had also become apparent to him, despite having only met her a couple of times, was he'd fallen completely in love with their daughter Kim.

At seventeen, she was a year younger than Calvert, slightly built and with a mass of unruly red curls which she was constantly at war with. At that point in time she still had the little gap between her two front teeth, a feature which he'd found most appealing, but also one she would have corrected shortly after the move to Mother City. Gifted with a zeal for life which never failed to amaze or amuse him, she'd purposely set about lifting him from the quagmire of depression and self-doubt he'd fallen into, gradually shaping him into what they would jokingly come to refer to as a 'normal' person.

Within six months she'd moved in with him, immediately redecorating the rooms, changing the drab browns and greys Calvert had originally chosen to warmer pastels. She bought brightly-patterned rugs for the floors, and hung curtains which complemented the new colours of the freshly-painted walls. Not for one moment would he feel put out by this; never once did he question her choice in anything.

A little over three years later, Elliot was born, and for the first time in his young life, Calvert felt complete. He now had everything he could have ever hoped for, and was finally ready to put the past behind him. In the months succeeding the birth, Kim busied herself with the new baby, seemingly content with the tasks of motherhood. Meanwhile, having found in himself a natural talent for repairing things, Calvert was inundated with work from the residents of Gunners Park.

Over the next few years, however, their idyllic life was to change. Kim, having grown tired of what she'd come to view as a rather humdrum lifestyle, was beginning to harbour feelings of resentment for what she would continually allude to as his "deep-rooted lack of ambition". While Calvert would readily admit to this, the truth was also that his level of energy had dropped and could no longer compete with hers. At other times, simply overwhelmed by feelings of suffocation he couldn't account for, he would look for any excuse to get out of the house. The stupid thing was he knew she would leave him—she'd, more than once, threatened to do so when her hints continued to fall on deaf ears. So why then had he not listened?

A dark-bodied truck grumbled passed, jolting him from his memories with a start. Shifting down noisily through the gears, it slowed to turn into the entrance of the AIR-Group premises before coming to a halt at the barrier. Here, an exchange of words took place between the driver and the night watchman, but Calvert was too far away to hear anything more than indiscernible mumblings. Eventually, the barrier lifted and the vehicle continued on its way through, leaving him to watch the red tail lights until they disappeared from view.

As a young boy growing up in the city, he'd held quite a fascination for lorries. At weekends, he would lean out of his bedroom window to watch them pass by, all different colours, with their big corporate logos emblazoned along the sides. For many years now, they'd all been black and unmarked—drearily identical and quite military-like in appearance. Unlike the modern day automobiles, they would fail to evolve very far. And so, much like the majority of his childhood infatuations, *trucks* were to become another which would quickly run its course.

One afternoon, when Elliot must have been about four or five, Calvert had taken him to the Metro Portal—the only official entrance and exit accessible to Mother City. Here, from a distance, they watched as the trucks thundered through the tunnel, their powerful engines revving and air horns blasting. On leaving, each one would pass through the checkpoint where the back of it would be searched, before gas masks would be allocated to the drivers and any crew, along with the requisite papers permitting them to leave. Likewise, on their return, the masks would be handed back in for sterilisation.

Calvert wasn't sure just how contaminated the air outside the city actually was—or even if it was at all—but he did have a vague recollection of once seeing a government article about a driver who had removed his mask, and his death was particularly unpleasant. The incident was big news at the time, replayed over and over again on Insight Extra, the official government news channel. Although deep down he believed the story to be a hoax, the horrific images did leave a lasting impression on him. 'Maybe that was the point of them,' Art had once suggested, when Calvert finally confided in him as to how much they kept preying on his mind. Whatever, despite the apparent risks, he often felt envious of anyone who was given any opportunity to leave the confines of the city—even if it was just for a few hours, cocooned in a vehicle and wrapped in a plastic suit fitted with breathing equipment. Like most people, he'd never been outside the walls, and the likelihood of him ever getting a pass to do so was next to nonexistent. They were rarely issued to citizens at his level.

Silence had returned to the proximity of the AIR-Group premises. Looking up, he saw the oval lights of the tall tower still burning an anaemic shade of yellow, too feeble to illuminate anything even in its immediate vicinity. Were they ever switched off? What business really went on in there that needed to be conducted under the cover of darkness, and why was Art O'Sullivan still so reticent to discuss or even acknowledge his part in its development?

'Sod it,' he muttered to himself, turning on his heel and heading in the direction of home. There were no answers here, just the usual mass of questions.

17

Art O'Sullivan had risen shortly after dawn, following what was quite possibly one of the most uncomfortable nights he could remember. Despite the exhaustion which would drag him prematurely to his bed, once there, sleep was slow to arrive and erratic when eventually it did. A combination of stomach pains and anxiety had kept him turning long into the early hours until, just as light was beginning to edge its way into the room, he'd finally given up any last lingering hope of rest.

Now sitting at his kitchen table, the usual sugar-laden mug of coffee in front of him, he noticed the stove had burned low overnight. Telling himself he would see to it later, he wondered how much longer the cold spell could continue for, bitterly concluding that by now, much like himself, it must surely be on borrowed time.

The sun was just starting to climb into a clear sky, casting long shadows across his lawn, where a frost now lay like a glittering white carpet. With the exception of the birdsong, all was quiet. Wrapping a blanket around his shoulders, he reached for his coffee and headed outside to the small veranda which he'd built to the rear of the house many years ago. Easing himself carefully into a rather ancient rattan armchair, he closed his hands around the steaming mug, grateful for the warmth it provided, wishing at the same time that he'd thought to take a piss before subjecting his weak bladder to the cold air. Sadly, these days it couldn't be relied on to function like it once had. But then again, he couldn't complain—it wasn't like he'd ever treated any parts of his body with respect. Whatever, despite his declining health, he'd still managed to get the truck to start at long last—at least he could tick that one off his list. He might not be able to repair the decay within his bones, but somehow he'd finally succeeded in sorting *that* battered old bastard out. Although it may have only one more assignment, it was to be a critical one. After that, like everything else in his life, its work would be done.

A sudden fluttering from behind Art's chair dragged him from his thoughts. Skewing his head around, he was surprised to find himself being studied by the beady, yellow-ringed eyes of a blackbird. Perched on the far end of the painted balustrade, its head was cocked curiously to one side, as though weighing up the situation—food, or no food? Danger, or no danger? After a little while, it seemed to sense he presented no immediate threat and began to cautiously inch towards him. Within a couple of minutes, it was so close he was sure he could have reached out and touched it. Yet he resisted the temptation, aware that if he stood any chance of befriending the bird, it would have to be done slowly, a step by step process—undoubtedly a lengthy process—and quite probably, a *more time than he had left* process.

Again, the blackbird tilted its head and stared towards him. This time Art couldn't help but see something comical—almost human, in the gesture. As he chuckled to himself, the sudden gruffness of his voice was enough to startle it, causing it to take flight. Slightly disappointed, he made a mental note to bring some scraps out tomorrow on the off-chance it might return. Pulling the blanket tightly around himself, he closed his eyes and turned his face towards the sun, enjoying the orange glow which filtered through his closed eyelids. Art had come to a decision; today he would talk to Marcus.

The resolve to do so had come to him in the early hours—for him the time when all such ideas were born. There were things that needed to be explained, a discussion which maybe should have been

136

held between them long before now. Not for the first time, he found himself questioning his own motives for keeping his friend in the dark all these years. Could he honestly put his hand on his heart and say it had been done for the sole reason that he believed it to be in Marcus' best interests to not know? Was it at all possible his silence had been really little more than a case of self-preservation, purposely avoiding a subject out of fear that, in his addressing it, he might also have to reopen a door to part of his own life—one which he'd been trying for the last thirty-odd years to keep tightly closed?

There was no way of spinning any other angle to it. He had failed in his duty, convincing himself that to say nothing was for the best. Telling himself in those early months, 'the boy is too traumatised to deal with it,' had seemed a plausible enough reason at the time—also one which would have gone a long way to appeasing his own conscience. As the years went by, it was to become replaced in his mind by 'he's doing okay now, so why rock the boat?' Still, he couldn't change the past, so there was little point dwelling on it at this late stage. What he needed to concentrate on now was the little future he had left, and how best to use it. Guessing it to be around 7am, Art was well aware Marcus wouldn't be up for at least another two hours. Two hours to reflect on how best to approach a subject he'd kept quiet about for the best part of thirty years—two hours to work out how he was going to address another that had come to his attention only yesterday. Starting to feel uncomfortable in the chair, he shifted position, aware of the dampness from the melting frost which was now seeping through his pyjama bottoms.

Like so often since his diagnosis, he once again found his thoughts returning to the question of his own mortality. How long did he actually have left? Come to think of it, how long did Gunners Park have left? Maybe they would fall together. This idea appealed to his sense of humour as well as his rebel spirit. He pictured himself like old man Darcey in Callingden, the last of the true breed fighting for his home; a hero to some, a pain in the arse to others. Not a bad way to be remembered; a synopsis he would be more than happy enough to see under his own name, if only that was possible.

HERE LIES A HERO TO SOME, A PAIN IN THE ARSE TO OTHERS
DIED FIGHTING THE SYSTEM

The last bit wasn't true, of course, but he reasoned it sounded a damn sight more interesting than *PASSED AWAY AFTER A LONG ILLNESS.*

At one point he'd seriously entertained the idea of going out in a blaze of glory like some modern-day Butch Cassidy when they finally did come for him, but had since dismissed the idea. Ten years ago, maybe, but these days he could hardly climb the stairs, let alone become embroiled in a shootout with the military. The reality was he would most probably just quietly slip away in his bed, quite alone and oblivious to everything, while off his face on painkillers.

Recently, he had felt the changes within him, the signals that time was running out, and wondered how obvious the deterioration was to others. Surely Marcus must be conscious of it by now, or were they both simply playing the same game, each pretending to the other that any day his condition might begin to improve? As with his own impending demise, he was struggling to come to terms with the news that time was also running out for Gunners Park. Although not yet officially, he'd been informed by a trusted source that by the end of the year it was to be torn down for redevelopment. Now Callingden had finally been swept from the map by the powers that be, rumours of large earth-moving machinery being spotted on the outskirts of Thornton Hamlet were already beginning to circulate—as good as confirming it had been earmarked as next in line to fall. There could be little doubt that Gunners Park, the largest of the three rural communities in Sector 21, would shortly follow—swallowed up by Mother City, only to be regurgitated as yet more concrete block and perspex. Once erased from the landscape, there was to be no further space allocated for future rural communities. Yet another unpleasant truth to add to the others—the ones he'd been keeping from Marcus for many years, waiting for the right moment, which of course there would never be.

In search of a more tolerable sitting position, he twisted himself around in the chair, and from the corner of his eye saw something that really had no business being there. From a point just above his fence, he was being watched. Not by a blackbird this time—it was now the red, optical lens of a Snooper which appeared to have taken an interest in him.

With their deployment to the outer reaches of Sector 21 having been stepped up over the last year, Art was more than aware that the occasional sighting of one patrolling Gunners Park during daylight hours was inevitable. However, their presence anywhere was something which had always greatly rankled him, and here he was not alone. Mobile Security Officers, although widely accepted within the populace of Mother City as a necessary contribution to the law and order of society, were generally viewed with suspicion and cynicism by most residents of Gunners Park. Art had often wondered how the public could have been so easily duped into believing the government's fraudulent claims concerning the purpose of *M.S.O.s*. To him it really couldn't be any more obvious that, other than spying and collecting information on individuals, there was no credible reason for their existence. However, they no longer held the same level of fear over him that they might have done in the past. For a moment he was even tempted to throw a stone at it, something he might not have contemplated a few years ago. One of the few advantages of dying, he'd recently concluded; you have so little to lose that you can do anything without having to live in the shadow of repercussion.

'Fuck off back where you came from,' he now hollered as loudly as he could manage, his middle finger raised in the Snooper's direction. 'Useless piece of crap! Don't you have anything better to do?'

For whatever reason, the machine withdrew its eye, before swivelling its turret to scuttle away, leaving O'Sullivan spluttering with the effort of the brief confrontation. A minor victory? Perhaps. Maybe not, but in an odd way there'd been something satisfying about it nonetheless. Shifting his weight from one buttock to another, he tried to push the incident from his mind and get back to thinking about Marcus, but the encounter had left him a little more agitated than he would have cared to admit. How long had the bastard thing been there watching him, and why? It couldn't be anything to do with the truck, surely? He hadn't used it for months. He racked his brain for a few minutes more, but was unable to find a plausible reason. Deciding that maybe it was time to retreat to the dying embers of his kitchen stove, he cast a final eye around the garden, only to see the blackbird had returned.

Enthralled, he now watched its approach: a few hops, then a pause before continuing, only to repeat the procedure again and again, until like before, it was only a few feet away from him. Art could see the bird was hungry, and was back to see if there were any changes in the food situation during the few minutes it had been gone. He wondered if he could tame it, maybe even get it to sing for him? Carefully rising, his movements as stealthy as he could manage, he crept back inside, taking a minute or two to empty his bladder while he was there. On the kitchen table, last night's bread and butter lay untouched, which he now tore into several pieces before making his way back to the veranda.

No sooner had he stepped outside, then from out of nowhere, a sharp blow to his left temple knocked him sideways. Stunned, he dropped to his knees, his palms pressed to his forehead, now certain the moment had come. *This is it, Art—bit sooner than expected, but there we are.* He realised he no longer feared death as he once had, only the possibility of being incapacitated.

But it was not his time. Unpleasant as the ordeal was, it was thankfully short-lived, the pain dissipating almost as quickly as it had arrived. Breathing deeply, Art clambered unsteadily to his feet, slowly straightened himself and looked around him. As he lifted his eyes, he saw the silver-grey, spherical head rise high above his fence, swaying from side to side on its gangly, flexible neck. The Snooper had returned, this time accompanied by two others, motionlessly positioned one on either side. For a while it just seemed to hang there, thirty feet or so above the ground with no obvious purpose, until eventually dropping itself down to stretch across the garden towards where he now stood glaring. Almost upon him it stopped short, and settling at eye level, cocked its metal head to one side, just as the bird had done earlier. It was clearly mocking him, but O'Sullivan was done. He'd neither the energy nor the will to antagonise it this time, certain the thing was responsible for the assault on him. Instead, he and the offending Snooper simply stared at each other, man to machine—machine to man—both calculating what the other would do next.

For quite a while, neither moved, until finally Art backed away.

'Checkmate, you fucker. Call it quits, hey?' he mumbled, reaching for his chair and dropping down into it. For whatever reason, the machine also conceded, retracting its neck little by little, until it had completely returned to the other side of the fence. Visibly shaken but unharmed, Art now watched with relief as the trio of M.S.O.s began very slowly to withdraw, although he would not allow himself to breathe easily until he was certain that this time they had actually gone. Unclenching his fist, the squashed bread fell from his fingers, reminding him of his reason for being out there. A little way from him, he could just make out the blackbird sitting beside his woodpile. His eyesight, although still good for a man of his years, was not as sharp as it once was and he'd failed to notice it at first. Tentatively lifting himself upright, he shuffled towards it, until finally he was as close as he dared to get. Looking down at the ground, he cursed loudly, before turning and disappearing into his house. By the woodpile, the bird lay dead.

18

AutoButler v.3.1.7 - The AIR-Group Pat. No. 84828723 -
Assignment GH-22

*Client log no. 9537 - **Scan no.** 6249*

***Body temp. check**/*normal* - **Pulse rate check**/*normal* - **Blood**
pressure check/*normal* – low scan continue – maintenance mode*
engaged

Results filed - continue medical itinerary - 24 hour monitoring

Once again the AutoButler ran through its most recent calculations,
before finally confining them to its memory banks. It was now 9:15am,
nearly thirty-four hours since its master's last session in the recently
deactivated chair, and for the first time that week, a marked
improvement in his health, mood and general well-being were clearly
evident. The Councillor's blood pressure had returned to a less
alarming reading, as had his previously rapid pulse rate.

It was with some degree of reluctance that he'd eventually agreed to
a medical itinerary being initiated, not at all happy at having anything
imposed upon him by a cybernated manservant. However, the results

spoke for themselves, and at present he was sleeping soundly, maintaining an encouraging average of fifteen breaths per minute.

Although not able to access Ocular Mode in either the bedroom or bathroom, the AutoButler was, however, equipped with the capability to audio-monitor, permitting it to track and analyse sleep patterns. These, too, had taken a turn for the better, especially in comparison to the grim findings of the previous week. If its calculations were correct—and they would be—the Councillor could be expected to return to normal equilibrium in a little under thirty-six hours, as long as he continued to recuperate at his present rate.

The doorbell rang. The six opening notes to the national anthem immediately alerted the AutoButler to the presence of an unexpected guest. Protocol now insisted the most stringent measures to be followed before admission could be permitted.

'Please place your hand upon the sensor pad,' it requested, the automated voice now only audible at the front door. 'I will alert Councillor Hurst to your presence.' With a quick scan of the visitor's fingerprints, identification was ascertained and a message swiftly dispatched to the sleeping Councillor's earpiece. 'Colonel Bramford to see you, sir.'

In those next few seconds, the AutoButler recorded levels of anxiety which it would spend the next hour thoroughly scrutinising.

19

Alerted by the AutoButler's message, Hurst sprang from the bed, his heart hammering in his chest. What the hell could that God-fearing sociopath Bramford want with him this early in the morning, and why hadn't the bastard called ahead to at least give him some warning? There wasn't time to dress himself; he would just have to make do with his house robe.

'Colonel Bramford to see you, sir.'

'Yes, yes, I know! I heard you the first time,' he barked angrily, tying the cord around his waist. 'Let him in, for fuck's sake.'

'Very good, sir.'

Furiously, he cleaned his teeth, defecated, and made his way to the lounge, where Bramford was already seated, alert and upright in Hurst's favourite chair. A well-tailored, navy-blue suit bearing the insignia of his church upon the breast pocket complemented a body toned and muscular from obsessive gym workouts. His skin boasted the healthy glow of a summer tan, leading the Councillor to momentarily wonder where such a colour could possibly have been obtained in what was being declared the coldest winter in nine years. In all ways, the Colonel wore his masculinity like a second skin, confident and at ease within it, every bit the alpha male that Gideon Hurst had over the years come to despise. The coffee cup he was now holding looked tiny in his huge hand, only serving to add to his already impressive stature. He took a final sip, before placing it on the white onyx table in front of him. Beckoning to the sofa opposite, his manner was more the conduct of host than guest.

'Ah, Gideon, take a seat, I trust you are well?' The smile was fleeting and lukewarm, failing miserably to reach his eyes.

Hurst dropped down onto the sofa, somewhat irked that Bramford had taken the liberty of instructing *his* AutoButler to serve him a beverage, something he himself would never have the impertinence to do, in the unlikeliness of the roles ever being reversed. Selecting a posture he hoped would suggest the relaxed demeanor of a man very much in control, he directed a gracious bow of his head towards his visitor and returned the greeting. 'It's good to see you, Colonel. To what do I owe the pleasure?'

Bramford cleared his throat and leaned forward, bringing with him a fragrance of mint mixed with expensive cologne. 'This isn't easy for me to say, so I'll cut straight to the chase. A few of us at the ministry have been a little concerned of late.'

Feeling his stomach turn over, Hurst opted for a perplexed expression, careful not to overdo it. 'Oh, concerned, sir? How do you mean?'

Looking around him as though to check they were definitely alone, Bramford shifted position in his seat. 'You don't seem to have been yourself for quite a while, Gideon. Is something bothering you? If so, I need to know.'

As though unwilling to trust himself with a verbal reply, the Councillor remained silent. Shaking his head, he busied himself with straightening some documents which were lying on the table before him, for no other reason than to avert his eyes from the Colonel's steely gaze, if only for a few seconds.

Bramford didn't look convinced. 'It's just that we need to be sure you're still a hundred percent on board. I'm sure I don't need to stress how important the success of this project is, or to remind you how much is financially invested in it. None of us can allow ourselves to become distracted by anything, not even for one minute.'

Hurst quickly pulled an excuse from out of the air. 'I have been a little under the weather—just one of those viral things. You needn't concern yourself, Colonel, I'm practically over it now.'

'Good, am relieved to hear it.' Bramford smiled weakly. 'And Calvert and O'Sullivan, have you served them official notice yet?'

Not at all comfortable with the direction the conversation was evidently about to take, Hurst chose the moment to instruct the AutoButler to make him a coffee, before remembering his manners and pointing towards the Colonel's cup.

Bramford declined with a dismissive flick of his hand. 'Well?'

'My man Deeks is presently informing all the residents of Gunners Park as agreed. But not Marcus. I feel . . .' The Councillor was beginning to look awkward. 'I feel that this one needs to come from me. As for O'Sullivan, I have personally obtained verification from M.S.O. data that he is not functioning at all well, very irrational displays of behaviour apparently. I really don't think he has much time left, to be honest.'

Immediately, Bramford's brow furrowed. 'It's not so much O'Sullivan I'm concerned about, it's Calvert. Looking at the intelligence gathered on him, and the little I've personally seen, I rather get the impression he isn't the type to just roll over, take the money and get the hell out. Is he aware that because of who his father was, he will be allocated decent accommodation in the city as well as being heavily compensated? I assume he has some inkling as to what's going on?'

Hurst hesitated, allowing himself time to consider his options—bare-faced lie versus truth—before deciding the former would very likely hold grave implications if discovered. 'Believe me, I have hinted at it,' he replied feebly.

'Hinted at it?' Bramford rocked back in his chair, eyes wide, his face darkening. 'Good God, man, we're way past that!' He softened a little. 'Look, I understand there's a connection—the son of your former business partner and all that—but really, this is no time for sentiment, Gideon.'

'Your beverage, sir,' cut in the AutoButler, followed by a short blip as the hatch on the opposite side of the room lifted, dispensing the coffee to the waiting silver tray. Relieved, the Councillor sprung to his feet to retrieve it, leaving Bramford frowning, clearly irritated by the brief intrusion to their conversation. Returning to the sofa, Hurst casually perched himself on an arm, anxious to display a sense of calm he certainly wasn't feeling. 'It's all in hand, sir, trust me. You have my assurance. Marcus Calvert will not be a problem.'

'He'd better not be.' The Colonel pushed back a shirt cuff to inspect the gold watch which encircled his thick, tanned wrist, before lifting himself effortlessly from his chair. 'These investors of ours, they're the big guns, you know—not the sort to disappoint. This needs dealing with now, no more *hinting*. The time for kid gloves has well and truly passed.' A solid, powerful-looking hand now came to rest on Hurst's shoulder. 'It pays to keep in mind that it's the Lord's work we do here today, Gideon, and as such, we are at his beck and call. Indeed, we must never forget that a civilised and moral society needs men such as ourselves fighting its corner. Twenty-four hours, no more. Forget O'Sullivan for the moment, we can always hurry him on a little.' The weak smile had returned.

At the door, Bramford turned to run an approving eye around the room. 'Nice place you've got here, you've certainly earned it.'

Hurst nodded, a modest simper crossing his face.

'And don't think we aren't aware or appreciative of everything you have done, Councillor,' he continued, only now choosing to address Hurst by his official title. 'It's all been noted and documented. We don't miss much at the Ministry, remember that.'

A fleeting tilt of his tanned head and Bramford was gone, leaving Gideon Hurst to wonder whether he'd just been complimented or threatened.

20

Squinting in the direction of the mantelpiece, Calvert was surprised to see it was already 9:45am, relatively early by his usual standards, but still a good bit later than he would have imagined. Although well over an hour since he'd crawled from his bed, his eyes were still heavy from sleep, watery and reddened behind his spectacles. Before him, yet another message to Elliot had just joined the others in a pile; like those too, it would remain unfinished. Calvert was not great with words at the best of times, and this morning, the ones he searched for were once again eluding him. Despite repeated editing, nothing would read as he wanted it to, until finally he'd given up all hope of writing anything that didn't sound either over-dramatic or simply pathetic.

When the knock at his door came, it was so muffled that, if not for the deathly silence which hung in the room, it might otherwise have gone unheard.

Suddenly remembering the walking cane he'd still not gotten around to returning, Calvert groaned in despair. Now certain the caller would not be anyone other than the Councillor, he cursed this oversight, one which could have so easily been avoided. True to form, and with no valid reason, Calvert had once again delayed in doing something, only to regret it later. The timing really couldn't be worse. But, almost as quickly as the thought had come to him, he was able to reject it again. The probability of Hurst turning up without prior formal notice was thankfully negligible.

It was then he noticed something different outside the window, just visible through the condensation upon the glass. Unless he was very much mistaken, it was the faded red roof of a pickup truck. Springing from his chair in disbelief, he hurried to the front door, fumbling with the security chain—and the lock he still hadn't oiled—pulling it wide open. Art O'Sullivan stood before him, a walking frame supporting his frail and stooped body. The black leather hat was pulled down low over his forehead, virtually obscuring his eyes; the familiar grey fur coat hung limply from his shoulders. It no longer fitted him as it once had.

'Take your time, Marcus,' he grumbled, 'it's bloody lovely out here, you know—did actually consider popping back home for my sun cream.'

'Art?' Calvert stepped forward, hand outstretched, his face unable to hide his concern. 'What are you doing here? Come on in, for God's sake.'

Taking hold of the old man's arm with one hand, and the walking frame with the other, he ushered him through his doorway, leading him across the room towards the chaise longue. For the first time ever, he was conscious of the fact that he was now the bigger of the two of them, something a year ago he would never have thought possible. Suddenly, reality hit him head-on, bringing with it a wave of sadness and missed opportunity. They could skirt around the issue all they wanted, pretend everything would be okay, but in the end it would change nothing. Art O'Sullivan was dying.

Calvert walked over to the kettle, not wishing his friend to see the tears which had formed in his eyes, needing those few seconds to clear them. As he set about preparing coffee, his back still turned, he heard Art clear his throat behind him. 'Forget that, Marcus, go get me a real drink. Oh, and one for yourself while you're at it—you look like shit.'

149

Despite the gravity of the situation, Calvert couldn't help but smile to himself as he grabbed a half-full bottle of whisky and two glasses from the small cupboard above the hob. Plonking them down on the coffee table before the old man, he was pleased to notice that, for the moment at least, he seemed to be comfortable. Fetching the low stool from its place beside the stove, he positioned himself opposite. 'I can't believe you ventured out on a day like this, Art, but it's bloody good to see you.'

Leaning forward, his forearms crossed upon his lap, O'Sullivan's stoic expression was giving nothing away. When at last he did speak, his tone was serious. 'We need to talk, don't we? I suspect there's much you need to know, and I guess now is as good a . . .' He shrugged, letting the sentence hang.

Calvert actually felt himself gulp. Whatever was on the old man's mind, this was unlikely to be an easy conversation for either of them. It was also one which, now finally faced with, he was no longer so certain he wanted to be having. 'We really don't have to . . . if you're not, you know, up to it.' It was a feeble reply and they both knew it.

'Ah, but we do—and I am.' Art laughed; a new and unfamiliar wheezing sound had now replaced the once-boisterous cackle. He pointed a finger towards the glasses. 'But first, you sort these buggers out—and don't be a stingy bastard.'

With a trembling hand, Calvert poured, the neck of the bottle clattering against the rims of the tumblers. Only when it was empty did he stop, the glasses now filled almost to their brims.

Art reached out and took one, waited until Calvert had done likewise, and chinked his own against it. Holding it aloft, he declared a toast. 'To the truth, the whole truth, and nothing but the glorious fucking truth.'

'The truth,' echoed Calvert, wondering just what form that might arrive in. He watched O'Sullivan knock back a swift mouthful and quickly followed, savouring the brief burning sensation within, promising himself they would do this again soon. There was still time—there would always be time.

For longer than felt comfortable, there was only the heavy whispering of his friend's tired lungs and the ticking of the clock on the mantelpiece to be heard.

It was Art who eventually broke the silence. 'Marcus, we both know I'm dying, so let's just get that one out of the way.' He held up his hand as Calvert moved to interrupt. 'I'm here to answer all those questions you have—that's all, not for any words of comfort or pity. There are many things you've never been told. Maybe I should've said them years ago, I don't know. Anyway, I'm here now so fire away. Anything, just ask.'

Calvert sighed. 'Well, obviously my father for a start. Who really was he—where did he go, and why? I hardly know anything about him.'

Closing his eyes, the old man paused as though to gather his thoughts. 'Your father . . . right. Yes, I did suspect we might be starting there. Marcus, before we go any further, there is something I need to be sure of, and please think hard before answering.'

A little surprised, Calvert leaned towards him. 'Of course, what is it?'

'Have you ever been chipped?'

'As in microchipped?' Calvert shook his head. 'No. Well, certainly not that I'm aware of anyway.'

'It would've been within the last fifteen years or so, as they didn't introduce it until sometime around '41. Think, when did you last have an injection for anything?'

'Ha, not since I was a kid—why?'

'Any surgery?'

'Er, no.' Again, Calvert shook his head. 'Art, what's this about?'

Lowering his voice in a slightly conspiratorial manner, O'Sullivan explained. 'Anyone chipped can have their side of a conversation listened to at any given moment. As you can probably guess, I'm clear too—so I guess we're good to go. Okay . . . your father. Well, as you already know, he and I were pretty close back in the day. Yeah, we

151

even went to school together, hung out most evenings. For many years I considered him a good friend, but I'm sorry to say, not always a good man.'

Calvert said nothing, his expression urging the old man to continue.

'I didn't see him for a bit; he went away to university to study psychology and criminology, that sort of thing. Hardly came back during the three years he was there. When he eventually did, he was sort of . . . I don't know—just different. Not only had he changed, but he'd also got that supercilious bastard Hurst in tow. I really couldn't take to *him*, and I'm damn certain he felt the same about me.'

'How do you mean *changed?*' Calvert was already intrigued.

'Big ideas—just kept on about mind reading, thought control, that sort of thing. How he and Gideon Hurst were going to "make serious waves" as he put it.' Art shifted himself, seeking a more comfortable position. 'I guess people do change over time, but your father certainly wasn't the fun guy I remembered from before. No, he'd become competitive about *everything*, and so damn serious. But anyway, they formed that partnership of theirs, set themselves up with a small research centre on the Hindenburg estate—you know, Outer Zones east. Well, that all worked out, and some years later they got that so-called *government payout* which took things to a whole new level. That was when I came on board. They got me in to oversee construction of the tower, which as you know, I did, and that was really the start of what was to become the AIR-Group. Two others joined shortly after me: Samuel Gorston and Dr Yvette Van Dijk.' His face clouded. 'Sadly, Gorston died a few years back, but Yvette is still there, even though she's passed retirement age now. She and I have stayed in touch; save for yourself and Kim, she's probably the only person I can say I actually trust.'

Calvert reached for his tobacco tin. 'You okay if . . . ?'

'Yeah, go ahead, knock yourself out,' Art chuckled. 'Not too concerned about my health these days.' He paused. 'A couple of years after everything was up and running, your father and I had a falling

152

out; I couldn't stay after that. No, I left the AIR-Group the very same day, never saw him again—well, not to speak to anyway. Gone, just like that, all those years of friendship down the fucking pan.'

'What was it about, Art?' Calvert looked up from rolling his cigarette. 'Why have you never said any of this before?'

'I buried it, mate, as you probably would have too. But anyway, you need to know this stuff so I'd better *unbury* it, sharpish.' The old man shuffled around for a bit. 'This is pretty unpleasant, so prepare yourself.'

Touching the lighter to his roll-up, Calvert drew deeply, before turning to blow the first lungful of smoke over his shoulder. Looking back at his friend, he nodded grimly. 'Okay, let's hear it.'

O'Sullivan cleared his throat, wiping his mouth with the back of his hand. 'Right, here we go then. So . . . this was the evening *before* the argument with your father, okay? It was pretty late—past ten for sure. I'd gone to the tower to collect something . . . one of those sleep gadgets, I believe. Anyway, the long and short of it, when I got there I found a dead body in the lift, lying there under a sheet on one of those gurney things. At first, I just assumed it was maybe some of the guys messing about—so of course, in I go, and get the shit scared out of me in the process. It was a bloody convict, no doubt about it, even had the prison overalls on. But his head, Marcus, never seen anything like it, all shaved and stitched up like something from a horror film . . .' He stopped, lost in thought for a moment.

Calvert stared at him until he caught his eye. 'Bloody hell, Art! So what did you do? Art!'

'Right. Yes, so anyway . . . the next day, off I go to see Valentine. He's in his office, and I tell him what I found, and—well, his reaction was not what I'd been expecting at all. The only thing he was concerned about was keeping it quiet. In fact, he good as threatened me with prosecution if I mentioned it to anyone—you know, all that disclosure of classified information bollocks. It was then he told me it was a new direction the company was going in, the removal of all thoughts and memories of prisoners, sucking their brains dry until nothing remained. Storing the information for research, apparently—and get this . . . *all* commissioned by the government. In my absence, Level Two had already been geared up for the sole purpose of this bloody *butchery*—and in his words, I "would just have to get used to it." Then he started laughing, like it was all just some big, hilarious joke. *Project Brain-Drain*, would you believe? No word of a lie, Marcus, that was the name he'd cooked up for it. Even asked me if I liked it—said he thought it was "catchy." Well, that was it for me, I'm afraid, I just saw red—completely lost it. Sorry to say I chinned the bugger.' A look of nostalgia crossed O'Sullivan's face. 'I can remember it like it was yesterday. Knocked him to the floor—broke two of my fingers at the same time. Anyway, I packed my stuff and security walked me to the door, and that was me done. The official story was that I'd had a mental breakdown. Not strictly true, but I let them run with it.'

Calvert stood up, unable to remain seated any longer. 'My father was involved in all this—not just involved, but a key player?'

'Yeah. Sorry, but I'm afraid he was. But don't forget, Hurst was also just as complicit, what with him being the technical mastermind, or guru—or whatever it is he likes to call himself these days. They were both as guilty as each other in my book. The only difference is that Hurst still is.' Art paused. 'You must have wondered what Level Two was for?'

'The second level of the tower, you mean?'

'Yeah. Nobody got to see in there—not even me once it was up and running, but that's where all the nasty stuff goes on. According to Van Dijk, it's pretty gruesome up there. She's wanted out for a long time, but the government won't release her. Gorston tried to walk away about six years ago, and look what happened to him. Suicide? Yeah, like bollocks it was. Anyway, where was I? Oh, yes . . . about six months, maybe a year after I left, your father just disappeared. Apparently, some pretty sensitive files and other stuff went missing too—or so I heard on the grapevine. Whatever, he vanished without trace, leaving that twisted fucker Hurst in control. You have to believe me, Marcus; I have no idea where he went—or why. Did his conscience get the better of him? If so, why did he leave you and your mother to fend for yourselves? Was he bumped off by the powers that be for acting so recklessly with their nasty little secret? It's possible—I really can't say, but nothing would surprise me. I do recall that at the time, Gideon was choosing to believe it was some kind of political kidnapping, but you know what he's like. In his eyes, Valentine could do no bloody wrong. So . . . sorry to say it, but I'm as much in the dark concerning what happened to him as you are. However, there is more to tell, and unfortunately, it only gets worse.'

'Worse, you say—how the hell can it?' Calvert moved to sit down again.

'Ah, we're both going to need more grog for this next bit, I can assure you.' Art held his glass up before him. 'Come on, what else have you got stashed away?'

Calvert went in search and came back with an ancient bottle of brandy he'd managed to find lurking, dusty and unloved, at the back of the cupboard. 'Sorry, but this is about the best I can do, I'm afraid.'

Art watched him pour—didn't even bother to ask what it was. 'Okay, here we go.' He leaned forward towards his drink. 'What would you say if I were to tell you that this is all one massive social experiment?'

'What is?' replied Calvert, confused.

'Everything. Gunners Park, Callingden, the city—the whole bloody shebang. The opioid epidemic, the toxic air—you name it. Even the Dredge Wars were engineered.'

'Hang on, that doesn't make sense. We had nothing to do with starting the Dredge Wars. Aren't you forgetting it was our country that was attacked first? *We* were the victims. I know I was just a kid, but I do remember it actually happening.'

'You mean you can remember *something* going on. Alright then, cast your mind back. Who started it?'

'Not sure. China or North Korea, wasn't it?'

155

'Not Russia then—Iraq maybe? Think, Marcus, think.'

Much to his embarrassment, Calvert realised he didn't actually know. 'I honestly can't remember. It could have been any of them.'

'Exactly!' Art's eyes shone, his expression bordering on manic. 'How about *all* of them, or maybe even none of them? Because, believe it or not, there is no difference. They are one and the same.'

Taking a long slug on his drink, Calvert finished it in one. 'Sorry, Art, but what you're saying here really doesn't add up.'

'Oh, but it does. It isn't religious beliefs or skin colour that divides us, neither is it barbed wire fences or oceans. It's wealth and power, and the sociopathic bastards who can't get enough of it. There never were any Dredge Wars, they never happened. Nothing more than a hoax to keep us all distracted. And guess what? It bloody worked.'

Calvert poured himself a decent measure of brandy, topped up his friend's glass, and tried to digest what he'd just been told. The old man was pumped up for sure, displaying none of the exhaustion previously witnessed. But still, what he was saying was hard to believe. 'Okay, if what you're telling me is true, then why? Who would gain anything from it?'

Art's eyes glazed over for a few seconds before returning to the question at hand. 'War has always been profitable to the few who pull the strings—and by that I mean the ones who hold all the *real* clout. How many times in the past have you heard politicians claim that there's no money to clothe or feed people, only for it to turn out that there's a bottomless pit of the stuff if some distant land needs obliterating? Any crisis that can be engineered to keep us at each other's throats *will* be, especially if it serves to keep the masses from seeing the bigger picture. See, the problem was, as technology kept on growing, so did the art of international cyber hacking. It became a bit like . . . have you ever heard of M.A.D.?'

Puzzled, Calvert shook his head. 'No, never—what's it mean?'

Art took another mouthful of brandy, screwing his face up in the process. 'Mutually Assured Destruction. It was a phrase coined during the Cold War which started in the 1940s, and wasn't even a war as such. Basically, it was a flexing of nuclear muscles between the superpowers, with not any one country being able to actually attack another, due to the possibility that they themselves would be fucked during the subsequent retaliation—get what I'm saying? So, there they were, locked in some stupid stalemate like two school bullies in the playground, throwing out threats, but at the same time also scared of getting kicked in their own bollocks. Well, in a way, it got a bit like that again, about thirty or so years ago. No country was able to attack another without fear of reprisals, but not nuclear this time around. No, what they all feared was dirt.'

'Dirt?'

'Oh yes. Thanks to the internet, the entire population had learned too much about what was going on, about how the system *really* worked. Some started to kick back—not much, granted, but enough to ruffle some big feathers. Information had become knowledge, and knowledge was fast becoming power. So the world leaders, along with the usual oligarchs and heads of banking cartels, of course, got together to end what they could see becoming a crisis—well, for them, anyway. The Dredge Wars were a hoax, sold to us all as a world conflict. One in which, we'd apparently wiped out each other's media infrastructure, not to mention millions of files containing sensitive data. How very fucking convenient. I suppose you could say Mutually Assured Destruction had been replaced with Mutually Assured Deception.' O'Sullivan smiled, obviously pleased with his play on words. 'Anyway, a lot of nasty shit was buried while the bastards distracted us with *that* one. It also provided the fuckers with a legitimate excuse to rid the world of the internet—something they'd been wanting to do ever since it started to work against them.'

'And all the world's governments just agreed to this?' Calvert sounded sceptical, struggling to believe what he was hearing.

'They would've had little say in the matter. Decisions like this are rarely made at government level. No, they're merely the gatekeepers, not the puppet masters as they'd have you believe. The ones with all the *real* leverage are The Circle of Suzerain.'

Noting Art's empty glass, Calvert pushed the remainder of the bottle across the table towards him. 'I can honestly say I've never even once heard of—what was that again?'

'The Suzerain,' replied Art, tilting his head to acknowledge the brandy. 'They might be few, but they hold sway over everything. Nobody—apart from themselves, obviously—ever knows with a hundred percent certainty who this group actually consists of. It really is that closely guarded a secret. One thing's for sure though: nothing is done without their say so. Every war, recession, depression, boom or bust—all played out from the shadows like some hideous game of chess.' He spread his hands wide for emphasis. 'Like I say, the war—it never happened. Well, not like they say it did, anyway. They just needed to have complete monopoly over all information, and make sure we no longer had the tools with which to question it.'

'So, if what you say is true, why isn't it common knowledge? Why aren't there mass protests?'

'Ah, well you know what they say: he who owns the propaganda machine chooses the words that it will speak.' Art shrugged indifferently. 'It's expurgation, nothing more, nothing less, and never been any different. But to answer your question, it *was* out there for everyone to see. Well, those who were awake anyway—practically shoved in our faces at times. Nobody cared, or if they did, they couldn't be bothered to question it. Ha. Here lies Planet Earth—killed by apathy. Think about it, Marcus. Even when actual proof of the bastards engaged in their heinous acts was plastered all over the internet, did it make a difference? Did the people all rise up shouting, 'hey, this is disgusting, enough is enough!'? Did they take to the streets in protest? No—they did fuck all. Oh yes, they may have ended up baying for blood, but only when it started to affect them personally. Then they started to rise up, saying, 'hey, you know what, I think we've been lied to!' *Quelle surprise.* You don't say? So now I keep quiet about this stuff—have done for years. You can't halt the wave of stupidity any more than you can change the tides, and I'm certainly done trying now. I've been laughed at—lost friends, even—just through what I know to be the truth. That's the only reward for getting this stuff out.'

There was a moment's silence as Art drained his glass. Hoping to steer the conversation back to where it had been before it veered off course, Calvert was ready with his next question. Unfortunately, he was a second too late, and the old man was away again. 'Have you ever seen the Nuremberg trials of 1946?'

'Yeah, of course. Well, extracts of them, anyway.'

'Did you ever look at them and think—how? Stripped of power, they looked like nothing. Just a group of pitiful, middle-aged men. 'Yeah, but that could never happen nowadays!' everyone cried, and I must admit, in my naïvety, I once believed it too—you know, that it was something that couldn't happen in these modern times. But what are modern times? There's no such thing, if you stop and think about it. The era each of us lives through at our own particular point in time can't really be anything else, can it?'

'I suppose not.' Calvert shrugged, by now beginning to wonder if his friend may have over-medicated himself. 'I guess I've never really given it much thought.'

'What I'm trying to say is . . . nothing ever changes, whatever we're told. Least of all the end game—it's not meant to. It's not *allowed* to. You see, the reality is that politicians, royalty—presidents, even—hold no superiority over us once that position of power is removed. It's not like they are wiser, or physically stronger—in many cases, quite the reverse. But for some strange reason, human beings seem to have this odd desire to kneel down and grovel at another's feet. Sorry, I seem to have digressed a little.'

Pouring the last of his own brandy into the old man's glass, Calvert set about rolling another cigarette. 'You said something about the toxic air being untrue? It's something I've long suspected, but was never

159

really sure if it was just me and my, you know . . . this stupid, paranoid brain of mine.'

'Yours and mine both, mate.' O'Sullivan nodded knowingly, lifting his eyes to meet Calvert's. 'Apart from housing yet more surveillance cameras, the purifying towers are empty—just dummies. There's nothing in them at all. The air quality is the same everywhere in Sector 21, whether it's here or in the city. It's all just the emperor's new clothes thing again. Keep telling people the city air is cleaner and they actually start to believe they can notice the difference. Next thing, they're telling their friends how much easier they can breathe since they moved to the Inner Zones, how their health has dramatically improved and other such bollocks. Like I say, it's all a scam. My guess is that even outside the Containment Walls the air is pure. In fact, I'm sure of it. The walls aren't there to prevent the toxic air from getting in—that's just bullshit. They're there for no other reason than to keep *us* from getting out.'

'Okay, okay.' Calvert leapt up, breathing out plumes of cigarette smoke. 'Just supposing you're right, it still doesn't make sense. Well, not to me, anyway.'

Art reached for his glass, drained the dregs, and beckoned for him to sit down again. 'When you were a kid, did you ever take a stick and mess with a line of ants—you know, prod them about just to annoy them? Yeah, of course you did, we all did. Well, that's what we are to these people, just insects scurrying about doing their bidding, to be used as pawns or cannon fodder whenever they see fit. Like I said, all one big experiment, and maybe for no better reason than to see how far we can be led down the garden path before we realise, but you can bet greed will be playing a big part too. You have to remember, Marcus, these bastards we're talking about are psychopaths, they don't see things as we do. Imagine a cartel of bloody monsters—evil fuckers who have everything yet know the value of nothing, and you might just get the picture. It's their fix; nobody is going to stop them from getting it. Carnage, suffering—death—all just collateral damage, simply a means to justify the end. Most likely even heightens the pleasure for them, who knows?' He shrugged, catching his breath before adding, 'it's a game—one forever tilted in their favour, and sadly, one your father and Hurst were up to their eyeballs in.'

'And you know this with total certainty, Art?' Even before Calvert had asked the question, he already knew the answer.

'I'm sorry, son, but I'm afraid I do. Remember though, whatever Gideon Hurst would like to have folk believe, neither of them would have been decision makers. As I said, there are levels far above them where the scams are orchestrated, so it's quite possible they had little choice in the matter—I couldn't say. What I am certain of, however, is that nothing is determined from down here, at our lowly level, whatever we're led to believe. It all just dribbles down from the very top, layer by layer, everyone accountable only to the bigger bastard above them. So, there we go.' He coughed into his hand. 'Do us both a favour, will you, and check outside. I know for a fact I'm being watched.'

Calvert left his seat and walked over to the window, looking up and down the empty tarmac to confirm their conversation was not being monitored in any way. At last he could feel the alcohol kicking in, although the effects were not enough to calm him. 'There's more, isn't there? Come on, tell me—what do you know about the opioids?' He turned around and looked at the old man.

Like some clockwork toy which had finally wound itself down, Art was leaning back against the arm of the chaise longue, vacantly staring at the wall opposite. 'Forgive me, Marcus . . .' His voice was now little more than a whisper. 'But it would seem as though my own fix is starting to wear off. Believe me, I've had more dope charging through my veins this last year than I ever did as a teenager, but anyway . . .' For a moment, he seemed to lose his train of thought before continuing. 'The opioid distribution, the AIR-Group, the pleasure bars; they're all part of the same thing, controlled from above—just like everything else is.'

161

'You mentioned an experiment? Exactly what are we talking about here, Art? Is this the Suzerain again?'

'Mind control—and yes. Oh, and before you say it's bullshit, stuff like this has been going on since the 1950s. This is how it works, so just bear with me please.'

Holding his hands up in surrender, Calvert returned to his seat. 'Okay, just tell me.'

'Basically, it's set up to run as a vicious circle—a never-ending loop. So: One. They flood the streets with cheap narcotics—in this case it's that Oblivion shit they're all taking. It's good stuff and the kids get hooked, okay? Two. They then take it off the streets, set up these pleasure bars and make them the only place you can get it—but still all under the pretence of it being an illegal activity, of course. Now, three. These bars have all been fitted out with booths which show the films, and these are loaded with subliminal suggestions. You're familiar with the theory of subliminals, I take it?'

Calvert nodded. 'I am, but I didn't think anyone bothered with them anymore.'

'Ha, it was banned years ago, despite them saying it was all just bollocks!' O'Sullivan seemed to pick up a little. 'But remember, at the time, they had to insert the messages to appear so briefly they'd be undetectable to the person viewing them, so the results wouldn't have been that great anyway. It's different with the films in the booths; there's no laws to govern them, so they can stick what they like in them. You need Oblivion, Oblivion is good for you, or . . . Oblivion will make you wealthy, live forever, good in bed—whatever. All this being soaked up by young brains, and without any restrictions. Are you with me? So the kids are there, watching these crazy films which are telling them to get this stuff into them. Then comes the real bastard—number four. They jack the price right up. Only thing is, now the poor buggers are hooked on the stuff, but don't have the cash to buy it. And this is where number five raises its ugly head.' The old man leaned forward on his elbows, rested his forehead between his hands and sighed deeply. Certain that what he was about to hear would be the pinnacle of their conversation, Calvert listened attentively.

'Marcus, the kids get the money they need to buy the stuff from selling off their memories. They're extracted under sedation and processed to film. Yeah—the very same films they're watching in those booths in the back rooms of the bars. Not just kids, older people too, but it's mostly the young 'uns, as they need the cash so badly for the gear. I'm sure you're getting it now? Where do you think this all takes place?'

The expression on his face was confirmation enough for Calvert. 'It's the AIR-Group, isn't it?'

'Afraid so. This is Hurst's department, Level One of the tower. I'll make this quick, Marcus. Don't believe anything they say about the memories being borrowed. They're stolen—gone forever. The more times they go, the more of their memories are taken away and replaced with seeds.'

'Seeds? Sorry, but I don't get it—what are you saying?' Suddenly aware that Art had begun to sway, Calvert rushed over, arms out ready, in case the old man toppled. 'Art, you okay? Do you need to stop?'

To his relief, he shook his head and continued. 'Simulant seeds. That's the name they give 'em. False memories, suggestions . . . whatever you want to call it. They're put back in to replace what they take away, like a cuckoo does with its eggs. It's not anything organic though—more a kind of digital Trojan Horse, I suppose you could call it.'

Calvert was horrified. 'And what exactly is in these things—these seeds?

'That's just it, Van Dijk says she doesn't know. She's not even certain if Hurst does. Apparently it's all still very much in its experimental stages. I must stress, none of this is Yvette's doing. In her own way she's as trapped as everyone else. For the kids, it's set up to be one miserable, unending cycle. Whatever they get paid just gets spent on more dope, so they'll be back time and time again. The rehab centres

163

on offer are run by the same bastards supplying the stuff in the first place, so obviously they're set up to fail. The sad irony is that at some point, the very film one of these poor buggers is watching could be made up from pieces of their own memories, and they'd never even know.'

For a while neither spoke, but it was obvious to Calvert that his friend was holding something back—something which was very obviously troubling him. When at last he did continue, it was with a tone more serious than Calvert could possibly have imagined from him.

'Marcus, Dr Van Dijk tells me your Elliot is signed onto this programme under a false name. It was her who carried out the procedure and she recognised him—no doubt about it. I'm sorry, but Yvette is a hundred percent certain it's your boy. What he's got himself into is something he won't get out of again—none of 'em do. He'll be erased of everything that makes him who he is. They'll only stop when there's nothing more to take. The big plan is for the next generation to be moulded into anything that might possibly benefit the Suzerain's purpose. They will remove *anything* that might have any possible emotional or intellectual value, and substitute it with these seeds. I hate to tell you this, Marcus, but he has another session in a few days' time.'

Calvert's head was spinning. 'What the hell do I do, Art? I have to do something—I can't just let this happen.'

Reaching a hand towards his walking frame, Art O'Sullivan grasped it firmly before raising himself unsteadily to his feet. 'Listen carefully, son. There's a way out via the Containment Wall, I always suspected it but could never prove it. The good doctor confirmed it to me yesterday in her message when she told me about Elliot—but first you'll need the codes in order to get through. Hurst has them, 'cos of course it was him who helped design the abominable fucking thing in the first place. Marcus, you find the bastard and make him hand them over. Then go grab your boy and get the hell out while you can—you got that? Don't delay; with each procedure you'll lose more of him.' Art let the frame take his weight, and shook his head sadly. 'I'm sorry to throw more shit your way, but if what I've heard is true, Gunners Park is to go the same way as Callingden very soon, so there really is fuck-all reason left to stay anyway. Believe me, if I was well enough to get out, I would. Now please take me home.' He handed Calvert a very worn key attached to an even more worn fob. 'The pickup's yours—I've no further use for it. Oh, and check the glove compartment, there's something in there you might need.'

21

Calvert's boots clicked loudly upon the bare, limed floorboards, as once again he wandered over to the only window the room had to offer. Lifting the blinds a mere inch or two, he peered through the gap towards the virtually empty street below. From here he could clearly see the pickup which was parked (or rather, had come to rest) immediately outside, one of its rear wheels up on the pavement.

This was only the second time in what must be twelve years or more that he'd set foot in Kim's apartment, and as on his first visit, he again found himself wondering if this was really her? If anything, it was smaller than Number 7, without even a balcony—let alone a garden to escape to. To Calvert's cynical eye, it was a faceless, third storey concrete box, not even blessed with ugliness to at least give it *some* possibility of character. No doubt, some would describe its interior decor as *minimalist*, the prints on the wall as *neoteric*, but he was unable to see past anything other than a resemblance to a prison cell.

For some reason that Calvert had never been able to figure out, any property within the Inner Zones commanded an exorbitant purchase price, even if it was little more than a bedsit. Anything in the immediate vicinity of a purification tower and you would realistically be paying up to half again on top—yet another aspect of city dweller rationale which seemed to defy all logic. Like before also, he was too agitated to do anything other than flit around the place, a little self-conscious of the noise from his boots, but unable to stand still for more than a few seconds. Although gagging for a cigarette, he was more than aware from past experience that Kim's disgust for this "filthy habit" of his would be met with not only a blunt refusal, but also a certain amount of reproach. No, he would wait until he'd said what he needed to and was back in the truck before lighting up.

The journey here, although relatively short and free from traffic, had seemed never-ending, his impatience only adding to his poor driving. He couldn't recall the last time he'd been behind a wheel, or even what the vehicle had been, but certainly it would have been something a damn sight easier to manoeuvre than Art's old truck was proving to be. For all its old charm, there was no denying the pickup was long past its prime.

The Snoopers had been out in force, lurking down side streets like hordes of silver-grey praying mantises, their turrets swivelling as they watched him pass. *Observing—Collecting—Reporting.* The pickup's presence inside the Zones of the city was a gross violation; certainly by now it would have become an object of interest. Each jump of the lights, every erratic turn, nothing would have escaped detection. Whether it was via the red eyes of Snoopers, or the satellites above, he would have been closely monitored, the data then transmitted back to the M.S.O. nerve-centre to be uploaded for inspection. Within twenty-four hours, a warrant for his arrest would be issued and his house raked through by the authorities. None of that mattered. It was all irrelevant now.

Kim was perched on the edge of a chic, yet uncomfortable-looking sofa, weeping into a handkerchief. The news of Art's condition seemed to have hit her harder than Calvert had been expecting.

'Honestly, Marcus, he didn't say anything the other day when I called him. Obviously I knew he wasn't well, but not . . .' She stopped short of actually saying it.

Once again, he was unable to find any words which might bring her comfort, too awkward to sit down next to her and hold her. Instead, he opted to stand just out of reach, rolling a cigarette that he couldn't smoke, and wait for the sobbing to cease. Only when she seemed to have composed herself a little, did he tell her what Art had revealed to him about the opioid spiral and the memory-forfeiting programme conducted within the tower. However, the look of disgust on her face would be enough to convince him to omit the part concerning his father's past involvement.

At his mention of Elliot's recent procedure and the full implications of what he'd signed himself up for, Kim leapt suddenly from the sofa and out of the room. As the sound of retching seeped through the wall, Calvert raised his hands to his ears. A couple of minutes later, pale and obviously distraught, she returned, now wearing a tan-coloured trench coat, a mass of toilet roll clutched in one hand. 'We have to get him now, okay? He needs to go to one of those drug rehabilitation places right away. Now, Marcus, *now*—you were supposed to be sorting it, remember?'

'Look, this isn't all down to me,' Calvert snapped back. 'Sorry, but you need to shut up and listen, okay? The rehabs don't work—they aren't meant to. This is no bloody conspiracy theory, it's fact. We do it my way as agreed.'

Kim slunk back to the sofa. 'So, what's *your* plan then?'

Calvert dropped into a matching armchair opposite her. 'I'm getting him out of the city, first thing tomorrow. Sorry, Kim, but that's how it has to be.'

'You can't. They won't give you a pass, and even if they did, it's twenty-eight days' clearance. Please don't tell me you think you can get through the checkpoint in that old thing out there?'

'We won't be going through the checkpoint,' Calvert stated flatly. 'We'll be going through the Containment Wall.'

Kim's face switched to an expression somewhere between annoyance and disbelief. 'Do you seriously believe—?'

He held up a hand to silence her. 'Just hear me out before you say anything, okay? You do know it was the AIR-Group that was commissioned to build the walls—whenever it was—thirty-odd years ago?'

'Yes, of course.' Kim shrugged. 'So what?'

'And that Gideon Hurst was technical director?'

'Obviously.'

Calvert chose to ignore the snarkiness. 'Well, according to Art, when Hurst designed the one for Sector 21, he added in an escape route—which of course he kept quiet about. I'm guessing it was his emergency get-out in case the shit ever hit the fan. There are codes to let you through. All I have to do is get them from him, pick up Elliot and get out of here.'

'Great, and what about me?'

Calvert stood. 'Look, you asked me to sort it—I'm sorting it. Sorry if it's not what you had in mind, but for once, I'm doing the right thing.'

'If he goes, I go too.' Kim's eyes narrowed, her chin jutting out in defiance.

'You'd leave Mother City, give up this place, your career and everything?' He swept an arm around the room for emphasis. 'It's different for me, I've got nothing left to lose. Art is dying and there's a rumour that Gunners Park is soon to be demolished. There's not exactly much left here for me anymore.'

'Like I said, if he goes, I go.'

'I have no idea what's on the other side, you know that?'

'Since when have I expected any guarantees from you, Marcus?'

Calvert let it pass. 'All I'm saying is—'

'Oh, I get what you're saying—you don't want to be responsible for me. Well, don't worry, you never really were, so no change there.' Kim's eyes flashed coldly at him.

It was at that moment, with that one expression—that bitter statement—something inside him died. Years of self-recrimination now fell away, as though some huge weight had just been lifted from his shoulders. For as long as he could remember, he'd mourned the demise of their life together, unable to move forward in anything that could be considered a positive direction. So much time had elapsed, with him clinging on desperately in hope of a reprieve—a second chance to put things right. Locked in a state of limbo, he'd become emotionally crippled by a past which nostalgia had allowed him to believe was perfect. The truth was simple, and at long last staring him in the face. He'd let her walk away because he'd grown weary of her; the black moods, the constant demands, but above all, the spiteful remarks.

'Kim, this isn't helping anyone.'

'Well, as long as it works for you, I guess that's the main thing.' Her tone was cutting—sarcastic. 'Thanks for clearing that up.'

Calvert had heard enough. 'Whatever, I really haven't got time for all this now, I'm gonna see Gideon and get those codes.'

'And then what?' Her return sounded more like a challenge than a question.

'As I said, I'll be taking Elliot away from Mother City first thing tomorrow.'

'Good luck with that, Marcus. He hardly knows you, let alone trusts you.'

'Nice one, thanks,' Calvert retorted. 'What do *you* suggest then?'

Kim rose from the sofa, her eyes red and slightly puffy. 'I can get him out of the flat. You just be there and . . .'

'And what?'

'Just . . . don't let me down, okay, Marcus?'

Calvert headed to the door, pulling it open. At the last moment, he turned and met her gaze full-on. 'Believe it or not, Kim, I'm not actually doing this for you.'

22

AutoButler v.3.1.7 - The AIR-Group Pat. No. 84828723 - Assignment GH-22

Client log no. 9537 - Scan no. 6250

Body temp. check/*normal* - Pulse rate check/*abnormal* - Blood pressure check/*abnormal* – Mental stability check/*abnormal* - continue low scan – maintenance mode engaged

Results filed - continue medical itinerary- 24 hour monitoring - particular attention to mental well-being

From behind its steel grating in the ceiling, the AutoButler's eyes turned from red to amber as it automatically shifted itself into Wake Mode. Having spent the best part of the afternoon resting in Semi-Sleep, upgrading and updating itself, it was well-prepared for any challenges that might await it. Woken by the activation sensors located on each side of the apartment's front entrance, it now watched as the Councillor threw open the door and strode over to the sofa. There he stood for a while, head lowered as if deep in thought, before dropping his leather attaché case down upon it. And then the restlessness began. To and fro across his lounge; boney, slippered feet virtually silent upon the white, handwoven rugs, his long arms folded across his chest.

Detecting levels of agitation well above normal, the AutoButler now began a series of adjustments—ones which had, in previous and similar situations, proved effective. Lowering the lighting, it now experimented with various colours before selecting a soft blue. A quick recap of its memory banks and immediately Mozart's Piano Sonata 16 in C major began to cascade soothingly across the room. Seconds later, a fine, single malt whisky made its way through the hatch towards the silver tray, where it was ignored.

Eventually, the Councillor seemed to tire. Throwing up his arms as if in resignation to his present dilemma, he collapsed upon the sofa, venting his frustration with a long sigh. Dragging the case onto his lap, he flicked the catches open to reveal pages of technical documents, on top of which were two white envelopes.

The AutoButler, programmed to procure—within reason—any information that could be used in assisting its master, immediately engaged Ocular Mode before zooming in with its telescopic eye. Scanning the print on the front of each envelope, it then proceeded to add the details to its data banks, instantly resulting in a match. Two names and addresses, plus a file on each, provided some basic background details, but little more. Methodical to the last, the AutoButler promptly engaged Archive Mode, a function which enabled it to replay any previous conversations which had taken place inside the apartment. Here, too, there was minimal information to analyse as the Councillor rarely entertained.

The only recent dialogue consisted of the exchange which had taken place between himself and Colonel Bramford just two days prior—a conversation in which the two names on the envelopes were mentioned. The AutoButler now fed all the details into its Anatomizer to dissect and analyse the discussion, before reaching the conclusion that there was nothing here to help it in performing its duties.

However technologically advanced it might be, it had exhausted all options available, and still failed to bring comfort to the Councillor.

Something was very different in his demeanor this evening, a level of sombre introspection never previously monitored by the machine, and very much outside the parameters to which it was confined. In its four years of loyal service, the AutoButler had observed everything, from outbursts of joviality through to absolute rage. It had calmed him on his return from challenging days at work, listened to his enthusiastic and lengthy monologues of his past achievements and future aspirations. On the rare occasions he'd been sick, it was there to advise and keep him supplied with the necessary tonics and pills while he convalesced. Yes, it would be reasonable to concede that the AutoButler was well-acquainted with most of the peculiarities of its master, but this particular mood was not at all in character with the man presently experiencing it. Indeed, this was a new but seemingly genuine response, and as such would need to be thoroughly scrutinised. The AutoButler checked and rechecked, before duly adding the word 'remorse' to its data banks.

23

Hurst was emotionally drained. Staring at the two white envelopes inside the open case upon his lap, he now searched his conscience for anything which could absolve him from what lay ahead. However hard he tried to justify his actions, he couldn't quite rid his mind of the feelings of self-reproach which had recently started to lurk there. Convincing himself it would all still be going ahead, with or without his personal involvement, was probably as close as he was going to get. He was also very aware that there could be no turning back. From the moment he put himself forward as official envoy—a title he'd readily accepted, and with much enthusiasm—the Suzerain had him firmly in their grasp. The moment a door to opportunity began to open before him, he'd stepped eagerly through it with little thought of the consequences. Not until the passing of many months would it begin to dawn on him that it was also a door which had since closed firmly behind him—a door unlikely to open again unless they, and they alone, were to sanction it.

Late afternoon, just as he was leaving the AIR-Group, he'd been contacted on one of his many devices by an extremely irate Colonel Bramford. The message—a little incoherent and peppered with expletives—was nonetheless clear on one point, one which for the life of him, Hurst could not conceive a plausible explanation for. Intelligence had just come in from numerous M.S.O.s that Marcus

Calvert had been detected driving erratically inside the Inner Zones of the city. The vehicle in question was an ancient and rather dilapidated pickup truck registered to an Arthur Eric O'Sullivan.

This made no sense to the Councillor at all; Marcus had never been a rash sort of man. Judicious as well as passive, he would be both aware and fearful of the penalties such an offence would bring about. Hurst threw down his case, the contents spilling out over the floor. For now, his work would have to wait. There was no possibility of him managing to settle down to it this evening.

In the corner, the still-disabled VS-2 sat ready to be returned to the AIR-Group research lab the following day. For a moment he contemplated re-coding it, losing himself in a world of deviant savagery for one last time. Had it not been for Bramford's thinly-veiled threats still ringing in his head, he would have probably thrown caution to the wind and surrendered to his vile urges. Instead, he just sat there, rigid—face hidden behind his hands, now forced to focus on an assignment he should never have committed himself to. But, however hard he tried, he seemed unable to keep his mind from straying towards his own thoughts—the ones which had recently begun to prod at his conscience, refusing to be ignored. It was now abundantly clear, even to a man as self-assured and egotistical as Gideon Hurst, that in accepting this commission, not only had he made a grave error of judgement, but was already in way over his head.

For a considerable time, the accumulation of wealth and privilege were no longer able to provide the stimulus they once had for the Councillor. Having achieved both long ago, they were now simply taken for granted, and typically, it was the pursuit of respect and admiration that continued to dominate his thoughts. Somewhat disillusioned with what he believed others viewed as an unglamorous and rather low-profile line of business, Hurst was adamant to set his sights a little higher. It seemed he'd dedicated the best years of his life to climbing the greasy corporate pole of success, spurred on by the assumption that, on reaching its pinnacle, his position within the upper echelons of society would be assured. But in truth, he found it to be an attainment which would not only continue to elude him, but slowly devour him also. What had in the beginning started out as merely a quest would, with the passing of time, end up becoming twisted into an all-consuming obsession, until little else in his life held any importance. Sitting at the top table with men of real influence and unquestionable power was, for him, the sole objective—his deserved and appropriate placement.

An ambitious and intelligent man by nature, his rise within his own particular field of expertise had been as predictable as it was impressive. However, it would never be enough to satisfy him. It was Hurst's personal belief that the pyramid of power was made up of five levels, with himself currently occupying the third, unable to climb to the fourth. Fifth level was, of course, Suzerain only, and therefore an impossibility. But reaching the fourth level—normally reserved for government officials and business moguls—was a realistic aspiration. It was also one guaranteed to bring with it not only prestige, but also an increasing dominance over others, something he continually hungered for.

In retrospect, he could now see he'd been used by Bramford (definitely a fourth level man) and his consortium of investors, picked not so much for his experience and skill at negotiation, but simply because his acquaintance with Marcus Calvert and Arthur O'Sullivan could be used to a possible advantage. The reality was that they didn't need his input now, and most likely never had. He was nothing more than a fall guy, a distraction—the people's focus for their anger and hatred when Gunners Park fell. In truth, despite his assurance to the contrary, Bramford would have been aware from the start that Hurst hadn't a chance in hell of talking either of the two men out of their homes. Success or failure, however, was of little consequence to them. It would be Hurst's name forever connected with the eviction and the levelling of an entire community—not theirs. He could see it now, carved into his headstone.

HERE LIES THE ARCHITECT OF DESTRUCTION
BETRAYER OF THE PEOPLE

Looking back, he'd always been the outsider, never really able to fit in anywhere. Even the friendship once shared with Valentine all those years ago never really evolved into the deep and meaningful one he'd been hoping for. *That* position was reserved for Valentine's one-time school friend and head plant engineer, Arthur O'Sullivan—something which had more than rankled him at the time.

Despite being well-educated and eloquently spoken, deep down Gideon Hurst couldn't help but feel socially inadequate when in the company of either of these men. Even worse had been the two of them together, which only intensified this misery for him. Theirs was a shared sense of humour which, however much he attempted to replicate, did not come naturally to him. In particular, he would feel continually undermined by O'Sullivan's sledgehammer wit, of which he often believed to be at his expense. Eventually the situation had become insufferable to him, and one he would try his utmost to avoid.

With O'Sullivan's resignation, later followed by Valentine's disappearance, Hurst had seized the opportunity to release the man he'd always wanted to be. No longer constrained by the fear of ridicule, he set about fervently changing his own self-image, banishing any thoughts of self-doubt and inferiority to the past.

In the subsequent years, now fully in charge of the AIR-Group and his own destiny, he would cross many lines, both legally and ethically, never once thinking to question his motives.

That was, until now.

24

Daylight had all but gone as Calvert swung into the floodlit driveway which led up to Councillor Gideon Hurst's apartment. On either side, purification towers, spidery and deceitful, sprouted from obsessively-maintained lawns, their secret still untold. Ahead of him, the ultramodern complex Hurst had called home for the last six years seemed almost surreal beneath the harsh glare of the levitating solar-lamps presently orbiting it.

No rusting pylons here, mused Calvert, leaning forward in his seat, as once more he attempted to wipe condensation from the windscreen with the sleeve of his jacket. With little regard for the mandatory 10mph speed limit or the groans from the transmission caused by his hit-or-miss style of changing gear, he now tore along the smooth, meandering asphalt before juddering to a halt outside the lofty entrance hall to Providence Lodge.

Although in the eyes of some it might have held a certain air of sophistication and refinement—no doubt the intention—Calvert's first impression of the Councillor's residence was that it was just another tasteless, self-applauding monument to wealth and excess. Yet there was nothing about its appearance which even remotely surprised him. From its vast expanses of tinted black glass, to the mock Roman pillars of glaring white marble, it was beyond ghastly and above ostentatious, just as he'd predicted it would be.

Switching off the engine, he checked all around him, noting the GlydeMaster was nowhere to be seen—hopefully an indication that Oswald Deeks wouldn't be either. Not that he was expecting any confrontation, but if the situation did happen to escalate, the chauffeur's presence could prove a possible inconvenience. Deciding to leave the keys in the ignition, he climbed down from the pickup's cab and into a quietness he would never have thought possible within the city's Inner Zones. Even Gunners Park, although a peaceful environment, was never silent to this degree; there would always be *some* noise, however unobtrusive. Immediately Calvert was struck by how unnatural it was to hear nothing at all, not even the hum of faraway traffic or the nearby twitter of birdsong. The fact that there was nowhere in sight for a bird—or indeed any other living creature—to inhabit didn't escape him either. Not one tree, hedgerow or plant for as far as the eye could see. Either nature was not welcome here, or it had chosen to give it a wide berth.

Just before the entrance hall's giant revolving door, he was greeted by a young and rather oily-looking concierge who, alerted by the pickup truck's clattering arrival, had come out to offer his assistance. Immaculately turned out in navy blue uniform and the shiniest shoes Calvert had ever seen, the young man declared that his name was Chauncey and ushered him inside.

The foyer was immense, floored in black and white checkerboard, and if not so dismally featureless, might have been quite spectacular. With the exception of a circular reception desk positioned dead centre, and the suave young man who was now taking his position behind it, the space was empty.

'You're Mr. Calvert, here to see Councillor Hurst, is that correct?' The voice had now switched from its previous smooth gushing to a more direct tone.

'I am, but I don't see how you could know that? He isn't expecting me.'

'Oh, but he is.' The concierge touched a finger to his nose in a knowing gesture. 'And, I think you'll find there isn't much that Mr Hurst doesn't know. Door two, sir.'

Calvert swung his gaze around the room. Four identical sets of doors stared back, numbers 1 and 2 to his left, 3 and 4 to his right.

'As you can see, there are four lodge apartments here,' the young man continued, now wearing an expression of pride, 'The Councillor is probably our most distinguished guest. Tell me, are you a personal friend of his?'

'Something like that,' replied Calvert, anxious to bring the exchange to a close. 'How do I get in?'

'The sensors will let you in. Unless . . .'

'Unless what?'

'Well—unless he's changed his mind, of course. Mr Hurst is quite a private gentleman, it's rare for him to entertain. He certainly . . .'

With a brusque thanks, Calvert prematurely ended the discussion and hurried towards the steel doors of apartment number 2, now greatly concerned the sensors might not permit him access; whatever else he'd prepared himself for, Hurst refusing to see him was a very possible setback he hadn't even considered.

Now standing before the entrance to the Councillor's apartment, he cursed under his breath. On both sides of him, rows of motion detectors blinked insanely, as though excited by his arrival. To his right, a circular panel displaying the illuminated depiction of a hand turned from amber to green, as an artificial yet strangely antiquated voice instructed him to place his palm against it. He now watched with growing impatience as the doors began their painfully slow opening procedure until, unable to wait for the mechanisms to complete their cycle, he shoved his way through and into the corridor beyond. Immediately he was greeted by the unmistakable sickly-sweet smell of disinfectant wafting up from beneath his feet, while from above, harsh white poured down from rows of glowing tubes. Laser beams—red and pencil-thin—now whipped across him as he walked, the absorbent, sponge-like floor beneath his feet releasing what appeared to be some kind of decontaminant onto the soles of his boots. Upon reaching the next door, an electroluminescent screen suddenly lit up, displaying one of the strangest messages he could ever recall seeing. It would confirm something he'd suspected for a number of years, yet had never taken the trouble to ascertain. In brilliant amber, the word *STERILE* now flashed repeatedly for about two or three seconds, before being replaced by a green *PLEASE PROCEED*.

Calvert was now in little doubt that not only was Hurst a borderline megalomaniac, but also a long-term sufferer of acute mysophobia. Here was a first-hand insight into what must be a miserable affliction to live with on a daily basis. What would have most likely started out as nothing more than cautious attention to hygiene, had obviously escalated to a stage where any sense of logic and reason would cease to exist. The possibility of contamination, however miniscule, was enough to dominate every aspect of this man's life. Suddenly, so much made sense; the obsessive glove-wearing, the polite refusals of tea or coffee when he visited—the out-and-out mistrust of anything that was not strictly under his control. In Hurst's world, not only would everything be clinically clean, but also closely monitored to ensure it stayed that way—scrutinised and sterilised over and over again. Anything less would be unacceptable.

The room he entered next was tiny, and save for a stainless steel box on a pedestal, otherwise empty. High up on the far wall was what he presumed to be some kind of monitoring system, from the centre of which, a massive eye was watching him. Slowly, as though weary from lack of sleep, it now blinked a heavy mechanical lid, before addressing him with the same voice he'd heard previously. 'Good evening, sir. Please allow me to welcome you to Councillor Hurst's residence.'

Even as a synthesised simulation, there was no mistaking the timbre of the man it had been configured to replicate, and now hearing it for a second time, Calvert was able to place it. With no suitable reply occurring to him, he just stood there nodding his head, his mouth gaping foolishly.

'Please forgive the formalities,' the eye continued in its educated burble, 'but I must now ask you to remove your boots and place them in the box.'

Calvert did as requested, wondering whether there was any way things could get more bizarre.

Now satisfied that protocol had been followed, the monitor finally permitted him to proceed, and a panel in the wall opposite slid open, beyond which a second corridor was clearly evident. 'Thank you, sir,' the monitor drawled. 'Councillor Hurst is ready to receive you.'

With its rubber flooring and white walls, the normality of this final passageway—especially in comparison to everything else he'd encountered since arriving at Providence Lodge—came as something of a relief. Now, as he padded silently along in his socks, he found himself wondering if Hurst also subjected himself to this same excessive level of screening, or whether it was reserved for visitors only. Ahead of him, a robust-looking wooden door began to swing inwards as he neared it, allowing him access into the Councillor's living quarters.

Calvert had never seen anything like it. If ever there was evidence of a man's damaged psyche, then this surely must be it. From every sterile corner, loneliness and desperation stared back at him, and for just a moment he was overcome with a great sense of sadness. Everything—the walls, carpets, even the furniture—all as pure white as any hospital linen. The same sickly sweet odour of sanitisation still hung in the air, although not as intensely as he'd experienced earlier. No pictures adorned the walls; not one ornament sat upon the bleached white shelves, their emptiness broken only by a solitary framed diploma. Taking pride of place in the centre of the room, a high-quality sound system sat upon a raised plinth, its polished surfaces gleaming beneath a strategically positioned spotlight.

A different Gideon Hurst from the one he had encountered less than a week ago now looked up at him from the sofa. Gone was the usual air of arrogance, now replaced by something which more resembled an expression of self-pity.

'You lied to me, Gideon.' Calvert was surprised at the steadiness of his own voice.

The Councillor frowned and let his gaze fall to the floor. 'Marcus, I have never lied to you, not ever. The situation is a complex one, and . . .' He paused, raising a finger. 'And yes, I confess that, on reflection, I could have handled it better, but I'm sure—'

'You think you could have handled it better?' Calvert interrupted, moving towards the coffee table which separated the two of them. 'You never thought to tell me about Elliot?'

The surprise on Hurst's face seemed genuine. 'Elliot? I haven't seen him for years. Sorry, Marcus, I can honestly say without fear of contradiction that I have no idea what you're talking about.'

'Councillor—let's just cut the crap, shall we? I know what goes on in that stinking filth pit of yours, okay? So tell me, what made you think it was okay to sign my son up for one of your disgusting programmes?'

'Hold your horses for just a minute, Marcus, let's stop right there.' Hurst had now risen from the sofa, his confidence returning; whatever else he was about to be accused of, *this* was something he was genuinely not complicit in. 'Firstly, the name Elliot Calvert has not appeared on any of our application or consent forms, and secondly, all procedures carried out on the AIR-Group premises are legal and approved by the government.'

Calvert narrowed his eyes, preparing himself for the angry denials. 'Even the ones carried out on Level Two?'

A look of amusement crossed Hurst's face and then disappeared. 'Ah, so that delusional renegade O'Sullivan has been getting things off his chest, I see. But in answer to your question, yes—*especially* the ones carried out on Level Two.' He waved his hand dismissively. 'But anyhow, let us not digress. I'm sure you're not here for a debate on the ethics of the work carried out by the AIR-Group? I can only reiterate that if somehow your boy has slipped into our system, it's without my knowledge or authorisation, in which case I can only apologise.'

'I want the codes, Gideon. You owe me that much at least.'

Hurst raised an eyebrow. 'Codes? Sorry, Marcus, but you've lost me once again.'

'As you said, Councillor, I'm not here for any debates, and I know about the codes needed to get through the Containment Wall, so let's just get on with it. I'm not looking to cause trouble, I just want to get my family out.' Calvert lowered his voice, choosing a different tact. 'Please, Gideon, this situation isn't good for any of us—yourself included.'

Hurst nodded thoughtfully, reaching a hand up to stroke his goatee. Calvert, looking at the pale, elegant fingers, realised it was the first time he'd actually seen the Councillor without his black leather gloves. The hand paused, dropping to join the other behind his back.

'And would this be for just the two of you . . . or three? And when, exactly?'

'The three of us—dawn tomorrow.'

'An unprecedented request, Marcus, as I'm sure you can appreciate. As such, it would have to be formally authorised by my superior, just so you understand.'

'I really don't care who authorises it, I just want the codes.' Calvert's voice rose, annoyed at himself for not even considering this possible complication.

'No promises, but . . .' Hurst selected his most sincere expression, 'you have my word I will give it my best shot. Now, if you will excuse me, I need to contact the Colonel.' Then, with a typical flourish, he left the room, leaving Calvert to nervously roam the white expanse, unable to stand still.

After what seemed like hours, but was in fact a mere fifteen minutes, the Councillor returned. In his hand he held a silver-coloured device, no larger than a cigarette lighter, which he now handed over. 'It would appear that today is your lucky day, Marcus. Your request has been authorised and the correct codes are, as of now, programmed in there. I have just personally uploaded them myself, hence the delay.' Returning to the sofa, he eased himself down with a calculated slowness and indifference, making himself comfortable before reaching towards the coffee table where a shallow pile of paperwork was neatly stacked. He flicked through a couple of pages before returning them, straightening the edges until they were parallel with the surface beneath. It was a gesture of arrogance, nothing more. Calvert might have gotten what he wanted, but he would be made to wait for instructions on how to use it. Eventually, Hurst looked back up and pointed to the tiny gadget in Calvert's hand. 'It's voice-activated,' he explained flatly, 'just speak into it when you set off tomorrow morning.'

'What do I say to it?'

Hurst's smile was a patronising one. 'Whatever you like, it makes no difference.'

'So, where do we get through?'

'When you get there, you will know . . . just follow the instructions as they come.'

Calvert inspected the device suspiciously, ever distrustful of anything he didn't understand. 'How can I be certain it will work?'

Standing abruptly, Hurst walked to the door, activating it with a wave of his arm. 'Remember, Marcus, as I told you not so long ago, our technology works for us—not against us.' He gestured towards the open doorway. 'Without wishing to appear discourteous, it really is time for you to leave. I have work to do.' The tone of his voice had changed. Any previous attempts at civility were now gone, replaced by a bitterness Calvert could not recall having ever heard before. If this was how it was to end, then so be it, he hadn't the time to question the sudden change in atmosphere.

Walking towards him, his hand outstretched, he attempted a final gesture of goodwill. 'Goodbye, Gideon, and thank you for doing this.'

Hurst simply nodded in reply, refusing the hand, choosing instead to turn his head away.

Calvert shrugged—it would appear there was nothing more to say. He slipped past him and down the corridor, resisting the urge to run. To his relief, the doors ahead of him were already beginning to open on his approach. He could see the box which contained his boots.

'Marcus, would you like to know what's on the other side?'

At the sound of Hurst's voice behind him, Calvert stopped and turned. The Councillor was staring at him from the opposite end of the corridor, framed in the doorway like some ghostly apparition, a lopsided smile across his face. His tone was mocking—a direct challenge—and for just a moment Calvert hesitated, tempted by a desire to know the answer. Shaking the thought from his mind, he took the last couple of steps through the hatch. Behind him, the door silently closed, but not before Hurst's taunting reply to his own question had followed him in.

'I'll tell you what's on the other side, Marcus. Nothing, absolutely bloody nothing.'

25

Calvert had woken earlier from a shallow sleep, cold and a little disoriented. For the last hour he'd just been lying there in the darkness, recalling the previous days and trying to make sense of it all. How had it come to this? It just didn't seem possible that his life could have been so ridiculously derailed in such a short space of time.

Self-doubt now began to eat away at him as questions he had no answers to crashed around in his head. Maybe what Hurst had told him was true, and there really was nothing on the other side? If so, what right did he have to put the lives of the three of them at risk like this—leading them through the wall like some modern day Moses? He certainly couldn't claim to be a saint, not even close—maybe not that much of a man either if his past endeavours were anything to go by.

Suddenly aware that his mind was dangerously close to straying into one of his *no-fly zones*, he sat up abruptly, telling himself to snap out of it—to empty his head of the negative thoughts residing there and instead focus his energy on the hours which lay ahead. Now was not the time for dwelling on past failings or indulging in self-recrimination. He was who he was, and if he had the capacity to change that, he would have done so long ago.

Rising from the chaise longue, he shuffled towards the table, reaching amongst the clutter for the few items he would need. Amongst them was the electronic device Hurst had given him, which he now stuffed into his jacket pocket. The carriage clock on the mantelpiece struck 5:30am and then fell silent.

This was it.

Calvert looked around him for one last time, knowing for certain that whether they made it through the Containment Wall or not, his days at Number 7 Gatling Drive were over.

Outside, a light flurry of snow had fallen whilst he slept, and he now checked for footprints, looking left and right along the road, relieved to see there were none. Closing the front door behind him, he took a moment to say his silent goodbyes, tracing his finger along the upside-down 7, briefly tempted to unscrew it and take it with him. An almost-full moon provided him with sufficient light to find a small offcut of wood in the pickup's cargo bed, and scrape at the layer of frost which had settled on the windscreen overnight. Now, as he tried the ignition and listened to the engine struggle to turn over, he was suddenly gripped by a new fear. The success of his plan rested on a rather tired, sixty-year-old truck, with a battery which had very obviously been weakened by the cold night's air. Pumping the accelerator a few times as he remembered seeing Art do in the past, his second attempt brought the pickup firing reluctantly into life. He found the lights and checked the dashboard's instruments, a little alarmed at the lack of movement from the fuel gauge. Tapping it hard with his finger, he swore loudly, feeling his pulse begin to quicken. How the hell could he have overlooked something as critical as making sure there was ample fuel? Whatever, it was too late to do anything at this stage. Maybe the gauge wasn't working? *Yes, yes, please let that be it, let it be broken.*

Grinding the pickup into gear, he headed as discreetly as possible along Gatling Drive, rounding the corner before pulling up at the end of Art O'Sullivan's driveway. Leaving the engine running, he walked to the front door and pushed an envelope through the letterbox, wishing he had it in him to bid the old man goodbye to his face as he deserved. He left Hurst's ebony cane propped up on the doorstep, figuring Art might put it to a far more worthwhile purpose than its legitimate owner ever would. A label hung from the silver handle, upon which was written a parting joke he knew would raise a smile.

Emergency accessory—nearly new—one previous narcissistic owner—to be used only during critical moments of extreme vanity.

Back in the truck, Calvert lifted a suede leather bag from the glove compartment and checked the contents, despite having already done so before his short nap earlier. Inside lay Art's pistol, the black metal rendered practically invisible within the darkness of the cab. Removing it from the bag, he was at once comforted by the gun's cold, heavy feel in his hand. He placed it gingerly in his jacket pocket, hoping he wouldn't need to use it.

Turning out of Gunners Park, he eased off on his right foot as he felt the worn rear tyres momentarily lose traction. Ahead of him the road sparkled as the beam from his headlights fell upon it. Patches of ice lay glass-like, blackened by the tarmac beneath and virtually impossible to detect until he was almost upon them. Descending Pilgrims Hill cautiously in third gear, he hunched himself forward over the wheel, his eyes straining to distinguish between reality and shadow. A convoy of shuttles sped by in the opposite direction, no doubt returning from dropping early shift workers at the factories, the glare from their headlights temporarily blinding him. Now approaching the Outer Zones, he turned left, heading past the industrial units which were already teeming with life. Beneath an array of flood lights and neon logos, bodies moved in all directions as minds became one, a microcosm he'd never been part of—a whole ethos he couldn't begin to understand. It was here where gears were oiled and potions boiled—lessons learned and fingers burned—wheels turned and denarii earned; a mysterious and alien jungle where he knew basic survival would be as much as he could ever hope to achieve.

Five minutes later, Calvert turned left again into Chester Green, a complex of small, government-owned, prefabricated flats built shortly after the millennium. Originally intended to serve the needs of the younger generation, they had instead over the years become something of a dumping ground for middle-aged winos and down-and-outs who, once there, typically progressed no further. It was a landscape of abandoned electrical appliances, graffiti, and ransacked bin bags left to fester and decay. A community tucked safely out of sight, lest it should blight the view of the privileged as they gaze from the windows of their opulent towers.

For once, the social injustice of it all was a long way from Calvert's thoughts as he now pulled up outside Elliot's apartment, relieved to see the light on, its glow just visible around the edges of the poorly-fitted blackout curtains. Now, he found himself faced with another dilemma. If he killed the engine, there was the possibility of it not starting again—however, to leave it running would deplete what might be precious last reserves of fuel. No, he couldn't risk running out. Besides, it should be sufficiently warmed up by now. Turning the key, he felt his stomach knot as the engine died. It was a decision he'd taken with uncharacteristic haste.

Jumping down from the cab, he ran the few steps it took to reach the front door, turning to look up at the night sky. Dawn was rapidly approaching, the blackness retreating, giving way to a dark shade of blue—the stars all but gone. Finding the door partially open, he pushed it as far as it would go, feeling the piled-up bags of rubbish stacked behind it give way. A smell of putrefaction greeted him as he walked the short hallway and into the cramped kitchen area.

Kim and Elliot were sitting opposite each other at a small, fold-down table. Amongst the debris of discarded pizza boxes, coffee mugs and makeshift ashtrays, one of her small hands reached out to her son, her voice soothing and calm. Now bearing witness to their obvious affection and intimacy, Calvert felt a stirring of jealousy within him and immediately hated himself for it. They looked up, acknowledging his arrival, but instantly returned to their hushed conversation.

He'd prepared himself for the worst, but even so, Elliot's appearance was disturbing. Admittedly, he'd hardly been the most sturdy of young men, but Calvert had never seen him like this. His face, hollow-cheeked and blanched, was barely recognisable, now partially hidden behind a scraggly beard and long, unkempt hair which hung in dirty clumps. Despite everything, he was smiling—a distant, hazy kind of expression which he now turned in his father's direction.

'Hi, Dad . . . what are you doing here?' His speech was slow and slurred as though intoxicated, his eyes empty. Lifeless.

Alarmed, Calvert looked in Kim's direction for reassurance. As though anticipating this, she had risen from her chair to beckon him towards the hallway. Now out of earshot of Elliot, she pulled a pill bottle from her pocket. 'Benzos.'

'Christ, Kim, how long has he been on those? I thought it was just that other shit he was taking.'

She looked away. 'They aren't his, okay? Actually, they're mine.'

'Sorry if I can't keep up here, but . . .' Calvert shook his head in disbelief.

'As I've said before, Marcus, what I do is no longer your concern. What *is*, though, is getting him out of here and into that truck, which thanks to these,' she rattled the bottle in his face, 'is now possible. So, are you going to lecture me now—or can it wait?'

Calvert let it pass. 'Okay, let's go get him.'

'No, I'll get him, you just need to make sure that thing out there starts.'

Before Calvert could reply, she had turned her back and was gone, leaving him irritated that, like on so many occasions in the past, she seemed to be taking control of the situation.

Now seated in the pickup, he turned the ignition, breathing a sigh of relief as the engine caught straight away. Reaching into his right hand jacket pocket, he removed the device Hurst had given him and held it to his mouth. 'Turn on now please,' he whispered into it, peering down between his fingers for signs of activity, his inherent pessimism already telling him to anticipate failure.

In those next passing seconds, Calvert experienced something that was beyond both his control and his understanding. It was as though everything within and without him ceased to exist; like some massive pause button had been pressed, held, and then released again. Like a sudden rush of water breaking through a dam, images and voices now began to pour into his mind. Faces he'd never seen, words he would have never heard spoken; all pieces of a life never lived, now merging with his own, before receding to leave only what was necessary for the task ahead. In his hand, a green light had begun to rise and fall, lazily blinking like some luminous reptilian eye. A shiver passed through his fingertips—a creeping sensation which progressed upwards along the inside of his arm, not stopping until it reached his forehead. He slipped the device inside the cuff of his jacket, pressed tightly against his inner wrist. And then he waited.

Elliot was the first to emerge, his steps short and hesitant like those of a late-night drunk returning home. Kim followed closely behind, head bowed, her shoulders hunched inside a white fur jacket. She climbed up into the cab, reaching down to help Elliot in after her. Closing the passenger door, she rested him against it, and began the futile search for a seatbelt.

'Not a chance, those are long gone,' stated Calvert, shaking his head. Leaning across them both, he pressed the door lock button down, recoiling from his son's body odour. 'Bye, bye, Chester fucking Green,' he muttered as he slipped the truck into gear and accelerated away, certain that whatever happened, he would never have to see this godforsaken shithole again.

Out of the estate now, and passing the factory units once more, Calvert soon realised he was being led to his destination without actually having heard a single spoken word, as one would when guided by their own memory. At every junction or turn he made, he was aware of the instruction entering his head, accompanied by other, less defined background thoughts which were very definitely not his own. Somebody had travelled this route before, even if he hadn't.

Before long, the paper-smooth asphalt of the city was replaced by the crumbling, pothole-infested bends of the backlands. Miles of dilapidated road surface, coupled with the uncertainty of what may lay ahead, were now beginning to take their toll on Calvert's already frayed nerves. Just as his mind began to stray towards the hip flask under his seat, he received another message—a change of direction was imminent.

A couple of minutes later, a densely-wooded area loomed up on his right-hand side, black and shapeless. At the last moment, he hit the brakes, skewing the vehicle around until they were facing down a narrow dirt track, all but hidden from view by the encroaching scrubland on either side. Only a pair of faint bald groves between the clumps of coarse grass left by previous passing tyres offered any indication as to its existence. He'd almost driven past it.

Cautiously he edged the pickup along, determined not to break the suspension having come this far. Somehow he knew they were now barely half a mile away—but from what, exactly? Checking the rear view mirror, Calvert noticed a black hover-car swing in behind, its distinctive, three headlight setup instantly recognisable as it followed from a distance. He turned to look at his passengers, relieved to see that, for the time being at least, neither were aware they now had company. Slumped against the door, not quite asleep but barely awake either, Elliot was still wearing the same expression of bemusement.

In contrast, Kim was a bundle of nerves, constantly twisting in her seat to look around, the confines of the cab restricting her field of vision. 'Is this it? Are we here?' she questioned nervously.

'Not yet, but nearly—only another five minutes.'

'How do you know, Marcus?'

Calvert wound down his window. 'I'm not really sure, somehow I just do . . . listen.'

Above the rattling and squeaking of the pickup, a deep droning sound now greeted them, steadily increasing in both volume and ferocity, the resonance of the lower notes felt rather than heard.

Checking the mirror once again, he muttered under his breath, noting the presence of yet another vehicle which had just joined the procession, tucking in discreetly behind the GlydeMaster. Although too far back for him to identify with any certainty, something about it suggested it was military.

26

Unhindered by the frozen, uneven surface passing beneath the hover-car's warm cushion of air, Deeks skillfully manoeuvred the GlydeMaster along the dirt track's many dips and turns. For once, sensing the gravity of the situation, he remained silent, wondering what was so important that it warranted him being dragged from his bed at such an ungodly hour. Leaning forward to deactivate the tracker's irritating audio updates, he checked the rear view mirror once again, but the origins and purpose of the vehicle which had just joined them and now followed closely behind were, as yet, a mystery to him. Up ahead of them, the pickup truck wandered erratically from side to side, seeking to avoid the worst of the ruts and the pockets of rock hard ice.

Dawn had broken to reveal a clear and blue sky. Just above the horizon, the first rays of a rising sun reached out towards them across the flat, frost-enveloped fields. In the distance, now barely quarter of a mile away, the Containment Wall stood defiantly—a translucent manifestation all but lost against the surrounding bleakness. As it weaved and shimmered, only the light now being reflected from its surface offered any suggestion as to its form.

As the convoy progressed, Deeks fumbled about on the dashboard, eventually finding a pair of expensive sunglasses which weren't his.

Admiring his appearance in the rear view mirror, he risked a sneaky glance towards his passenger at the same time.

Occupying the rear centre seat, Hurst was hunched forward, stiff-faced amongst the white velour and leather. Despite the efficiency of the heating system inside the hover-car, his arms were wrapped around his body like someone battling to keep out the cold. Since setting off from Providence Lodge nearly an hour earlier, he had hardly uttered a single word. As motionless as a shop mannequin, he now stared out between the two front seats, as though mesmerized by the truck ahead.

Drawing near, the dissonant moaning from the Containment Wall was enough to penetrate even the virtually soundproof interior of the GlydeMaster, causing Deeks to reach into the centre console for the earplugs he would sometimes slip in place when Hurst wasn't looking. Despite having been this close to the wall before, the chauffeur had never quite gotten used to the battering the subsonic frequencies could inflict. Hopefully, whatever was about to occur here, the Councillor would get on with it and they could be on their way again.

Ahead of them, the pickup's brake lights came on as it ground to a halt, and Hurst finally broke his silence, pointing to a spot about a hundred feet from where it now sat. 'Pull over there. Kill the engine and say nothing. Is that clear?'

No response.

The Councillor leaned forward, barking into his ear. "I *said*, is that clear?"

Without replying, Deeks did as instructed, intrigued as a hefty military vehicle now pulled in beside them. From within its rear door, a smoked glass window crept down to reveal two men seated inside. The one nearest to him had to have been at least ninety years of age. His face, although a healthy enough colour, looked drained of life, the skin beneath his eyes puffy and reddened—a face which was hard to believe had ever permitted a smile to settle upon it. It was nobody he'd seen before, unlike the man sitting beside him, now deep in discussion with one of the soldiers in the front. Although by no means a stranger to him, Deeks had initially been thrown by the black military beret he was presently wearing. Before today, he'd only ever seen Bramford in civilian clothing.

Hurst moved himself from the central seat to the left in preparation to exit the hover-car, his finger poised above the door activation button. 'Anything you see happen here today is carried out in the interests of national security—is that understood?'

Deeks nodded, his curiosity now well and truly piqued.

Hurst continued. 'And I can assume you are aware that the release of such information would be declared a criminal act?'

Once again, Deeks nodded. 'Of course, sir. I understand.'

'Good. Just wait here.' Immediately, the volume of noise from the wall escalated as Hurst's door slid open and he stepped out onto the frosted grass.

Hurriedly closing it again, Deeks settled back into the seat, any previous desire to leave now forgotten. Hidden behind the liberated sunglasses, his beady little rodent eyes stared out over the dashboard at the three people presently climbing from the pickup. Marcus Calvert, he instantly recognised, but who the woman or the filthy-looking kid were he had no idea. One thing he was certain of, however: whatever was about to go down, his employer was being leaned on—and if in any way that could be used to his own advantage, then all the better. He removed a tiny camera from his top pocket and waited.

Information was power, after all.

27

Calvert watched Hurst's long, thin frame emerge from the GlydeMaster and saunter over to the military vehicle which had just pulled up next to it. A darkened window dropped down a few inches; the face which peered out through the gap was featureless—certainly impossible to read at such a distance.

Looking back towards Elliot, Calvert saw he'd now raised his hands to his ears in an attempt to shut out the low rumble of infrasound. The first signs of awareness were already evident; he would have to act fast before the effects of the medication wore off entirely. Grabbing hold of his arm, Calvert began to lead him in the direction of the Containment Wall, taking his weight as he slipped and stumbled on the hardened earth. With his free hand, he removed the device from inside the sleeve of his jacket, at the same time glancing over his shoulder towards where Kim was following. For some strange reason, he found himself struck by how old she suddenly looked, her eyes wide with terror—her lips pinched tightly together. At that precise moment in time, he could have been looking at a complete stranger. Beside him, Elliot's step was slow and hesitant, yet he moved forward without any resistance to his father's grip upon him. His face was deathly-white, glowing with perspiration despite the cold air.

Now only about fifty feet away, Calvert pointed the device ahead, relieved to feel its vibrations once again. Before him, blue and orange light danced and crackled, forking its way upwards, weaving hypnotically through the distorted, undefined mass of the wall. An unexpected change in the wind's direction flicked a rising column of acrid smoke into his eyes. Instinctively he tried to close them, but it was as though they had been filled with sand. By now, the pungent fumes were beginning to lie heavy in his lungs, burning the back of his throat, the taste bitter upon his tongue. He pushed his thumb down hard upon the tiny button . . .

Nothing.

And then, all of a sudden, the noise dropped in volume—not completely, but enough to hear Hurst's voice cutting through. Now assisted by a loudhailer, it was the same mocking tone he had used the day before, only this time amplified.

'Marcus, whatever is wrong? It should have opened by now.'

Calvert turned his head, and through the dust and tears, watched as the Councillor leaned towards the heavy-set man in army fatigues standing beside him, legs spread as though poised for action.

As the man nodded in his direction, Hurst lifted the loudhailer to his mouth once more. 'Hold on, the cavalry is on its way.'

Letting it fall to the ground, he began to stride towards where the three of them stood huddled together. As he approached, his expression was one of mild amusement; never once did he avert his eyes from Calvert's. At only a few feet away he reached a gloved hand inside his coat and withdrew a white envelope. Now upon them, he presented it to Calvert with a brief flash of his lopsided smile, raising his voice to be heard above the resonance beside them. 'Just a small parting gift, Marcus. Please forgive me, but in all that drama yesterday, it completely slipped my mind.' He turned his attention towards Kim and Elliot, acknowledging their presence with a polite nod of his head. 'So nice to see a family reunited after all these years. Very touching.'

Without replying, Calvert tore the envelope open, quickly scanning its contents before rounding on him. 'What the fuck is this?' he demanded, angrily waving it in his face. 'You're here to give me a bloody eviction order? It's hardly relevant now, is it?'

Hurst shrugged. 'Maybe—maybe not. You see, Marcus, the next few minutes will determine that. Call it a social experiment, if you like.'

Now beginning to panic, Calvert decided to change tact. 'Please, Gideon—we really don't have time for this.'

'Oh, but *I* do, and I think you will agree, that's what is relevant here.' He paused. 'Let me explain. In just two minutes from . . .' Raising his hand, he waved it in a display of annoyance. 'Now, Marcus, please don't interrupt—this is how it's going to work, so listen very carefully. As I was saying . . . in two minutes from now, I will activate the wall, but—and here's the rub—unfortunately there has been a slight change of plan and it will only allow two of you through. But anyway, what I—'

'You backstabbing bastard!' Calvert stepped towards him, his fist clenched. 'You low-life, backstabbing bastard!'

Without even flinching, Hurst pointed over his shoulder to where two men in black now stood before the military vehicle, their guns raised in anticipation. 'Careful now, Marcus. The Colonel's men can get a little twitchy, so let us all just keep calm here. Right, so where were we? Oh yes—two of you only.' Hurst stroked his goatee thoughtfully. 'Hmm . . . decisions, decisions.'

Kim tugged at Calvert's sleeve. 'Marcus, he can't do this—please tell him he can't.'

Hurst swung around to face her. 'Ah, Kim, now that is where I have to correct you, I'm afraid. Actually, he *can* do that. In fact, *he* can do anything *he* damn well pleases. You see, Kim . . .' From his pocket he withdrew a similar device to the one he'd previously given to Calvert, holding it up for her to see. 'Unfortunately—well, unfortunately for you, that is—this one overrides the one Marcus has there. But as we have already established, we are wasting time here, so let us talk options.' He turned back to Calvert. 'Whatever you think about me,

Marcus, this really is not my decision, and never was. Do you really believe I would want *this*? If so, you really don't know me at all.'

'Just say what you have to say, Gideon, and let's get this done.'

The Councillor nodded, looking at them all in turn. 'Very well. As I have just stated, only two of you can go, but . . .' He smiled apologetically. 'At least you get to decide which two, so . . .' A gloved finger now hovered before his face. 'Option one: Kim and Elliot go—Marcus, you stay. Don't fret, we can soon find you accommodation.' Before Calvert could speak, a second finger had joined the first. 'Option two: you and Kim go and Elliot stays here. Just think, it could be like old times, Kim, before it all got boring for you.'

'If you think for one minute I would leave him here . . . what kind of—?'

'Now, now, Kim,' Hurst jumped in, cutting her off mid-flow, lifting a finger to his mouth. 'Please hear me out. Option three.' He paused, now raising up three fingers. '*You* stay here, Kim. You know, give the men a little bonding time together—let them catch up a bit.' He turned back to Calvert. 'Never forget, Marcus, that *she* took him away from *you*. All those years without him, was that *your* choice? Who knows, if Elliot had stayed with you, he might never have gotten himself into this predicament to begin with. Certainly worth considering, wouldn't you agree?'

Kim moved forward, now only a couple of feet away from Hurst. 'Forget it, Gideon, there is no way he's going anywhere without me.'

Stepping backwards, Hurst flicked a hand dismissively in her direction. 'All very touching, Kim, but you don't get to decide, I'm afraid. Only Marcus gets that choice.' He smiled slyly. 'How does it go again?' Spreading his arms wide in a thespian manner, he raised his voice an octave as to mockingly emulate that of a woman. 'Just don't let me down, okay, Marcus?'

As Calvert's mouth fell open in surprise, the Councillor flashed him a twisted smirk. 'You see, Marcus, *you* might not have been microchipped, but she was. Isn't technology such a wonderful thing?'

As the one uncovered eye bored into hers, his smile was cold—his voice measured. 'Yes, Kim, that little gap in your front teeth, remember? The anaesthetic you so willingly invited into your bloodstream? Oh dear, oh dear.' Once again, he looked towards where the heavy-set man stood observing the proceedings. Nodding at him, he turned back to Calvert, raising his hand in front of him to display the device. 'Time's up, Marcus. Don't keep us in suspense.' Brandishing it above his head, he then pointed his arm in the direction of the wall, as though he were a swordsman preparing to advance. With his head held high and chin thrust out, it was Hurst at his most theatrical—his grand finale.

Behind him, a change in sound caused Calvert to spin himself around. The wall's previous flat discord was beginning to oscillate, gradually mutating into a steady but persistent rhythm. He now watched, as like fabric being torn in two, it slowly began to part, until a narrow passageway had formed.

Hurst smiled. 'Sorry, but two minutes—that's all I'm permitted to give you and then it closes. So make it quick, and do *please* choose wisely.'

Kim grabbed hold of Elliot's shoulders, pulling him tightly to her as tears began to well up in her eyes. 'Marcus, I beg you, don't take him from me.'

Gently, Calvert prised his son away from her, throwing his arms around the frail body—their first physical contact for longer than he could remember. 'Don't forget me, Elliot. I know I should've done better and you've no idea how much I regret that. Maybe this is all that's left I can do to . . . to make it up to you.' Calvert choked back a sob, the words seeming to stick in his throat. 'I have always loved you and always will, but now you have to go. Both of you—just go.' Pushing Elliot away from him, he gestured towards the waiting portal. 'Kim, take him. Just . . . go now, please.'

As though rooted to the spot, he stood motionless, numbed from shock and cold, watching with dismay as the two of them walked away, taking their final steps out of his life.

Just before the wall swallowed them up, Kim turned to look at him for one last time. 'Thank you,' she mouthed.

And then they were gone.

He continued to stare after them, unable to turn away, almost expecting that at any moment they might return.

In those few seconds, he'd all but forgotten the Councillor, still standing beside him, now in communication with someone via his wrist gadget. Severing the brief conversation, he looked up, his face serious. 'I must say, an interesting choice, Marcus. Not the outcome I would have put my money on—but there . . .' He hesitated. 'I'm afraid I have some rather sad news for you.'

'Really? You do surprise me,' Calvert returned bitterly.

Hurst's expression was one of great forlorn. 'It concerns Arthur O'Sullivan. I have just been informed he was found hanged about an hour ago. A suspected suicide, but unfortunately no note. I really am very sorry, Marcus.'

Pointing the device towards the Containment Wall, he leaned in close to Calvert, as once more the level began to increase. 'Well, I think we're done here. So much to do, so little time, as they say.' He laid a gloved hand on Calvert's shoulder, squeezing it, before starting to walk back to the GlydeMaster.

A loud crack filled the air as a bullet ripped through his shoulder, causing him to cry out loudly in pain. As he dropped down onto one knee, he twisted his head around to look behind him to where Calvert stood, ashen-faced. Before him, a small black pistol lay in the mud.

In those final fleeting seconds, as the Colonel's men again raised their guns, Calvert closed his eyes and waited. Death was now a certainty, and he realised he no longer cared, but hopefully it would be quick.

As the clatter of gunfire split the February dawn, Councillor Gideon Hurst slowly raised himself up from the ground, brushed down the long black and blue leather coat, and walked away. Above him, a new sun looked down, its warmth already starting to thaw the frost beneath his boots.

Spring had finally arrived.

Epilogue

Outside the clubhouse, Elliot leaned back in his chair, savouring the April sun upon his skin. In the weeks since first arriving at the village, he'd changed beyond all recognition. The facial hair was long gone, and at last his skin finally had something resembling a healthy glow to it. The biggest improvement, though, was his weight. Despite still being a little on the thin side, his face was beginning to fill out, losing some of its haunted appearance.

The first week had been the worst—although he had little memory of it, aside from the occasional flashback. Most of his knowledge of what he'd recently been through had been gleaned from his mother and the four villagers who'd picked them both up immediately this side of the Containment Wall.

On a small, cloth-covered table to his left, two elderly men were deep into a game of poker. One of them—solidly built with a neatly trimmed, white beard—chuckled as once again his companion threw down his cards and passed him a cigarette, which he would then add to the growing collection before him. Elliot smiled to himself, certain the bearded man was cheating, and had been since the start of their game.

From the clubhouse, the sound of a guitar drifted towards him, soon accompanied by raised voices and clapping. He thought he could hear his mother's laughter and wondered if she was with Ralph Haslemere again (or Haz, as she insisted on calling him). Whatever, he was pleasantly surprised at not only how easily she had adapted to the alternative lifestyle of the village, but also the enthusiasm with which she'd chosen to embrace it. As for himself, he had to admit he missed the fast pace of city life, but overall, things here could be much worse.

According to 'Haz', the population was only about eight hundred or so, but larger settlements had also been established nearby. There were few laws, but a breach of them could result in expulsion if ruled so by the 'elder statesmen', a council of nine who acted as both judge and jury—of which Haslemere was one. Despite the simplicity of life here, there was running water, good sanitation, and electricity via the wind generators. Everyone had work of some nature, enough food, and wooden cabins for shelter.

Elliot rarely thought about his father, and his mother no longer mentioned him—it was almost as though he'd never existed. On some days, he would feel confused as to who he really was. At other times, convinced there were voices talking to him within his head, he would find himself questioning his own rationality. It was always the same message, whether real or not, telling him to come back to Mother City and that, in time, he would be instructed on how to do so. For the moment, though, he was content enough here, although the idea of going in search of one of the other villages was something which would occasionally cross his mind.

Next to him, the poker game had fizzled out. Scooping up his winnings from in front of him, the bearded man rose from the table, extending his hand out towards Elliot. 'You're new here, I believe?' His voice was deep with a pleasing tone.

Elliot took the hand. 'Yeah, I got here a few weeks ago.'

The man smiled broadly. 'First things first. Let me introduce my good friend, Felix.' He turned and gestured towards his smaller and rather morose-looking companion, who now nodded in acknowledgement. 'And me, my name is Valentine . . . Valentine Calvert.'

. . . and so we watch from behind the wire

Forgotten objects of desire

Apathy our only crime

An invisible army lost in time

Printed in Great Britain
by Amazon

65188063R00125